Sparky the Spunky Robot

Dani Brown

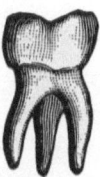

Bizarro Pulp Press
an imprint of JournalStone Publishing

Bizarro Pulp Press books may be ordered through booksellers or by contacting:

Bizarro Pulp Press, a JournalStone imprint
  www.BizarroPulpPress.com

  Print ISBN: 978-1-947654-87-7
  Ebook ISBN: 978-1-947654-88-4

Printed in the United States of America
JournalStone rev. date: February 22, 2019

Cover Art: Mikio Murakami

Interior Formatting: Lori Michelle
  www.theauthorsalley.com

Edited by: Scarlett R. Algee

Proofread by: Mike Thorn

I'd like to thank Em Dehaney for the name and title. Without it, I would have written an entirely different book. (Unfortunately the person of the keytar doesn't want to be mentioned, can't imagine why.)

1

In the dead of the night, while the rest of the house dreamed the sweet dreams of a moderately well-to-do family with only two overdrafts between them, Matthew liked to wander into the shed of his lost dreams and jerk off over his keytar. He could have been big, hanging on the tail end of British synthpop, but the condom broke. She wasn't on the pill. He hung up his keytar and replaced it with disposable nappies and regret.

His band went on without him, earning a top ten hit and a slot on *Top of the Pops*. In hindsight, it was best he didn't appear on *Top of the Pops*. Thinking of it made Matthew shudder, but it didn't make his balls shrivel.

Shoulder pads made way for unwashed shirts. Hairspray was bad for the environment. He could have been big. Everything about the 80s was big.

Life went on. Life went on when the baby slept through the night, and through the fall of the Berlin Wall. Life went on when Matthew found himself promoted to office manager in a job he couldn't describe with any level of accuracy.

Life went on when Karen fell pregnant again. And again, a few years later. She refused the pill. Didn't want chemical hormones messing with her body. Matthew secured packets of it, crushed it up and put it in her drinks. The idea struck him too late to save his dreams.

The keytar spent those first few years in a box, moving from mouldy rented flat to mouldy rented house. Matthew would take it out every now and then to press the keys and turn the knobs in silence. Karen wouldn't allow anything else.

When they bought their first place, his wife sent it into the loft with the record player and the black and white television set. He spent over an hour up there with it, knowing he wouldn't see it again for a long time. Karen ended up banging on the ceiling with a broom handle to make him come down again.

By the time their firstborn secured a scholarship with glowing marks on her plus 11, the family had upgraded with a tidy profit. Karen wouldn't allow Matthew access to any of that money. It was so they could have something in the bank and pay their children's way through university. Not because she was generous, but to show off in front of the neighbours.

Matthew's keytar once again went to live in the loft, away from the rest of the family. Karen didn't want to expose the children to creative ambitions. She wanted to give the neighbours the impression of a sensible family. They only ever had sensible hopes and goals. She never considered how Google factored into this life.

He put his foot down when his wife wanted to sell it at a boot sale for a fiver. The keytar was his first (and only) true love.

She tried to sell it again when the firstborn went to university. Matthew found himself in the local garden centre later that same day, purchasing the shed and paying for it to come pre-assembled. He used his secret nest-egg.

When he first picked up the keytar, he swore he wouldn't turn into his father, sad and alone day after day, painting gnomes for the neighbours in the shed. Keytars weren't gnomes. The gnomes had names. The keytar didn't.

He used to call her Sally, but not since he'd moved her into the shed with a selection of wires and metallic plates and random pieces of plastic. It reminded him too much of the gnomes.

He had to walk past them on his way to the shed each day. His father would bring a new one each time Karen invited him over for Sunday lunch. They delighted his wife.

Matthew liked nothing more than to kick them over and hear them shatter so he could replicate the sound on his keytar's half-sister, the tiny synthesiser Karen didn't know about. He kept it hidden in a drawer beneath a stack of old *Playboys* when it resided in the house.

His wife noticed they were gone in the morning. Matthew soon learned to leave their ashes and blame the wind, or the hedgehogs everyone in the neighbourhood fed.

His balls sagged to his knees. The stars twinkled down, urging him to ignore the throbbing longing and kick over a few garden gnomes.

His orgasm would be brighter if he shoved the stupid pound-shop plastic flamingos up their arses, broke the sticks off, and put them in their eyes. More of them appeared every evening when he arrived home.

Karen's fascination with lawn ornaments forced the angry vein to become a permanent feature on his forehead, even if it wasn't entirely her fault. She had to keep up with the neighbours in the hierarchy of garden decoration.

He went to his former peers' nostalgia tours, only to discover they were either still pretty, or their record labels provided the best plastic surgeons and makeup artists. Those who didn't have record labels had an army of menopausal followers willing to put towards whatever crowdsourcing pleas crossed their social media newsfeeds.

All Matthew had was his bloated balls, his dusty old keytar, and Karen. His frumpy old wife contributed to the crowdsourcing campaigns and Suburban Hell's lawn ornament addiction. His life wasn't meant to turn out the way it had.

There were little things he worked on, but nothing compared to being a faded star of yesteryear. He was meant to have a gold record and a big house on the hill, with all the other aging stars.

He kicked a ceramic gnome as jealousy gripped his heart and turned it a shade of green. The vibrations went through his balls, causing them to droop a little lower. Any further, and they'd fall to his calf to rub away the thick dark tangle of hairs.

The anger rose as the weight of his balls hunched his back. He kicked another gnome and bent to pluck a plastic flamingo out of the ground in the same painful movement.

He waved the flamingo like a magic wand. It didn't make his balls shrink. It didn't make his life the way it should be.

He discarded it in the smiling face of a gnome, missing the eye due to his balls sending a painful reminder of their existence. He wanted to kick it, but he needed a different sort of relief first.

Karen didn't care for the sex he offered, not since that stupid book or film or whatever with all the bondage and the abusive rich guy. Her selection of vibrators interested her much more than her husband's bloated balls.

Karen had her plastic boyfriends; Matthew had his gorgeous keytar, her curves as beautiful as when he first took her home. Karen grew frumpier each time she pushed out a kid, and with their passing birthdays each year since Matthew put an entire pack of crushed-up birth control pills with a heaping spoonful of sweetener in her tea and kick-started menopause.

A little pre-cum escaped into his y-fronts. It didn't take the ache away from his balls, drooping far below their torn elastic. Instead, it served as another thing for Karen to complain about. She hated washing sticky underpants, even more than she hated skids.

Sometimes Matthew ordered vindaloo on days he felt his balls escape below the ancient elastic prior to second breakfast, one to either side, for the simple fact it pissed her off.

Matthew's keytar called, his erection finally tearing right through his trusty old tightie-whities. They did nothing to contain his balls. He might as well switch to boxers, but Karen wouldn't allow it. Not as long as he kept his keytar. Only when it was gone would suburbia allow him to switch undergarments.

He unlocked the shed under the watchful eyes of the lawn ornaments. His wife tried to bury it beneath climbing roses, but something inside kept her at bay. Matthew pulled the string to switch on the light. Electricity in the shed offered something else for Karen to complain about. The neighbours didn't like it.

One of her vibrators met with an unfortunate accident when he found he could no longer cope with the nagging. Bigger than his cock, they offered no competition for his heavy balls.

Inside the shed, he transported himself to a time when shoulder pads and big hair were all the rage. Even Karen told him to get with the times. He could hear her voice now, as he listened for the night sounds of other failed musicians practicing in their sheds. He couldn't make out the words.

His keytar waited for his caress. He couldn't play her until he found enough money between the sofa cushions and dug up from the playground to pay for soundproofing. Karen and her army of lawn decorations wouldn't be the only ones to complain.

Matthew never could afford to convert a large farmhouse in the country. Some failed musicians went on to become important CEOs of big companies, but not him. He couldn't make it through the day without two things: jerking off, and Karen's incessant voice nagging him to the point he would put his hands over his ears and shake his head, appearing crazy to the person dishing out the promotions.

Instead, he was stuck in suburbia with neighbours and their twitching curtains. Karen's voice would've followed him into the country, even if he cut apart her body and flushed it down the toilet.

He ran his fingers along the keytar and licked the keys for a few snatched moments of pleasure. Pre-cum leaked into his underpants. His cock throbbed, calling to be sucked by menopausal fangirls high on anti-depressants and painkillers.

He took off his pyjama bottoms and hung them over a railing he'd installed when the shed arrived. He bought them special to house his dick (about average size) and his overfilled, aching balls. They were in better shape than his underpants.

The tattered remains of his stained y-fronts, he threw into the corner. The spiders were welcome to them. It would keep them from weaving their webs over his keytar during the day.

2

Too much cum would break his keytar. He allowed himself to blow his load over her only once per calendar month, except in December, when he'd allow for twice due to the festivities driving him insane. He had exactly two weeks to go before he could shower her in creamy man-juice.

He didn't need tissues or socks. Matthew constructed himself something better. He named him Sparky. The name had a ring to it that 'Cum Bucket' lacked.

Sparky wasn't a bucket, although his head was constructed out of a children's sandcastle pail Matthew had picked up in the toy shop. The pound shop sold the same buckets for half the price, but Matthew didn't want to run into his wife. She'd demand he take her to lunch when he needed to spend his lunch hour buying parts and jerking off.

The cum shots sprayed all over his shed before Sparky came to him in a dream one winter's night as salty snow fell every time he opened the shed door. Karen thought all that hairspray he used in the eighties had decided to come back and haunt him as dandruff.

He looked at the ceiling as he unscrewed the lid on Sparky's special compartment. The years-old cum made the shed cavelike. Karen kept purchasing upmarket dandruff shampoo for his thinning hair due to all the flakes on his pillow. The dust landed on his keytar.

He kept yellow cloths in a drawer for that very purpose, but first, he needed to see to his balls. He sat Sparky on the table and put him in a clamp.

Fairy lights served for the eyes he'd cut in circles in the plastic head. They turned on at the flick of a switch on the battery pack.

He had yet to give Sparky a voice. There was enough equipment left over from Matthew's failed dreams to build something, but he wasn't ready to give up the synths yet.

Time ticked. Each night, relief took longer.

He placed Sparky's lid on the table and looked into the hole cut into the robot's back. Each night, he blew his load into it, minus the nights he jerked off onto his keytar. Each night, the tubing emptied somewhere.

One Saturday afternoon, Matthew took Sparky apart. He couldn't find his spunk. The hole cut into Sparky had been lined with layers of latex and a little squirt of tingle lube. He fingered it to make sure it hadn't grown teeth in the twenty-three hours he'd been away.

Pre-cum fell from his dick and landed on the floor, in the same place it always did, building up a stalagmite. His feet became comfy in the grooves moulded into the floor next to it.

Matthew grabbed Sparky by the plastic bucket handle and pretended it was the robot's neck. Synth music played an endless loop in his head. It could have been a different song by a different band, but by the time he was on the scene, they all sounded the same.

Matthew's balls spasmed. They weren't ready to give up their cream. Matthew held Sparky still and thrust in and out with his hips. His balls hit the underside of the table, swung around with the motion, and hit his knees. Karen didn't buy dandruff shampoo for his balls.

Sparky's eyes flashed, one after the other, then went dead as they chased each other in his bucket head before lighting up again. Rats fought over bones left over from a family bucket of chicken in the alley. Even Suburban Hell residents liked their fried chicken.

The moment before orgasm had always been Matthew's favourite. All of his senses were heightened, moreso since he'd moved his keytar into the shed. He would, once again, think of rats as he came. They were becoming an issue.

Sweat beaded on his body and hit the air with a slight springtime chill to ensure he didn't overheat. Matthew saw ice crystals in his mind.

His wife's flowers closed against the night, leaving an aura of death as they slowly decayed with the amount of spunk in the soil. Since the shed, she could never keep anything alive for long.

Matthew pumped, his pants and groans travelling around the shed to hit his ears with slight distortion the second time he heard them. His balls contorted, ready to release their fluid. He increased his speed.

The way his balls hit the table and then his knees offered the slight bit of pain he needed to climax. The bruising carried him through the day until he could spend time with Sparky and his keytar again.

He blew his load, listening to the family of rats gnawing on chicken bones in the alley.

Cum leaked out of Sparky's lined hole, enough to drip onto the table. Sparky would be empty and clean by the next night. Matthew set up CCTV in the shed. It malfunctioned, leaving nothing apart from snow and white noise.

The shed seemed to break anything digital. After his second smart watch, Matthew started taking them off when he climbed into bed.

He spent his Sunday mornings at car boot sales, searching for old motion sensor recording equipment.

His balls wanted to go again. He knew it best to obey. He couldn't risk his job by getting caught playing with himself in the toilets again.

He bent down to look in Sparky's hole. Man-juice dripped out. The hole retained most of it.

It wasn't the time of month to caress his keytar. He used to be able to time it to visits from Karen's Aunt Flo, but not since Aunt Flo sighed her death rattle. These days, he kept a calendar and marked the dates. Two long weeks before he could turn the keytar over and jizz all over her backside.

Sparky sat, his eyes flashing, absorbing the juice of his father. Matthew didn't notice the change in the flashing. He was too busy trying to make it rain man-juice on the spiders in the corner.

Sparky turned his head. Matthew didn't notice. He wanted to cum until he shot dust.

Sparky watched his father with indifference. Any more sperm tonight, and he'd become too fat to support himself on his tumble-dryer hose legs.

Matthew's spare hand reached around to caress the keytar. Sparky's eyes glowed bright for a few seconds of solid light before he gained control. All of Matthew's anger and jealousy coursed through Sparky's plastic parts.

Rubbing the buttons and knobs on the old keytar forced Matthew's balls into convulsions. Jizz didn't flow out in a graceful river as it did into Sparky. Some shot out.

Then, a pause.

Matthew's balls contorted between his legs. Tears welled in his eyes and dripped down his cheeks. His balls squeezed themselves as he pulled on his foreskin and caressed his keytar.

The stage lit up. People shouted his name. The supermodel he'd been parking his dick in gave him a kiss with promises of more, if he could build a time machine and land in 1985. She pushed him onto the stage. The crowd broke into a frenzy. His fans were crazier than what the butt rock bands attracted.

His cock erupted. Matthew panted in the corner of his shed. The only audience were the lawn decorations. He could feel their plastic eyes watching through the treated wood. His keytar rested, silent and wondering if she'd ever be played again.

Matthew wiped jizz from his hand with a cloth as the dust welcomed the fresh fall of man-juice. He needed a moment to catch his breath and return to reality.

The boards of wood replaced the screaming crowd. He could have been big. He wiped his eyes with the cum rag.

Sparky looked like he moved.

"You watching me, big fellow?"

Matthew patted Sparky on the head. Even plastic had more affection for him than his wife. Sparky wouldn't mind if he played his keytar.

With a sigh, Matthew pulled his spare dressing gown off the rusty nail it hung from. Karen would be horrified if he ran through the garden and back into his house naked. Jizz rained on his pyjamas. He wouldn't be able to wear them again until he could get them washed.

She didn't understand how his balls could tear his piss-stained y-fronts and ruin the elastic. He really needed some new supportive underwear, but he'd rather save for a new computer and software. The millennials made their albums on computers without any instruments. His wife wouldn't allow him to drain the savings to cover the costs of having records pressed, but he could upload files to streaming sites and maybe even earn a few pounds.

Karen wasn't thoughtful enough to buy him a new pair of underpants.

He left Sparky on the table next to his keytar and locked the shed behind him. The flamingos and gnomes looked like they moved. Twenty-five years ago, he didn't think he'd have a garden covered in lawn decorations. He sighed. He could feel his balls starting to sag already.

3

Sparky glared at the keytar next to him. He knew she didn't get bathed in life-giving spunk as much as he did, but he watched night after night as Papa caressed her while grabbing Sparky's neck. He wanted to kick her off the table.

His tumble-dryer hose legs lacked the strength. His fingers touched her silent keys. Beneath the plastic case, she still worked. Plugged in, she'd be stronger than him.

Sparky wanted her parts. Sparky wanted Papa to view him as something more than a jizz deposit box. If he took the keytar parts to have a voice, Papa would never forgive him.

Papa wouldn't be the only failed pop star living on the street. The roads in suburbia were lined with broken dreams. They kept the houses propped up. One pill per day to bury it deep inside.

Sparky leapt off the table. He had surprisingly good balance for a robot with legs composed of tumble-dryer hose and arms made with vacuum-cleaner hose. His fairy lights rattled inside with the landing.

He gave himself a moment to catch his bearings. Sparky had never left the shed before.

The keytar wouldn't tattle; she was silent without electricity and an amp. Not even the monthly splattering of Papa's spunk would give her life. She needed electricity.

Sparky reached with his hoover arms for the spare key. He could open the lock by jamming his fingers inside, but he didn't want to destroy anything of Papa's. Papa's immense paranoia about Karen locking him in meant there was a key hanging inside the door. The advantage of being constructed out of two types of hoses involved being able to reach instead of jump.

Sparky didn't want to alert the lawn ornaments. His feelings towards them were the same as Papa's. Sparky stepped out of the shed and locked it. A sudden breeze would make the door bang and wake Papa. Sparky didn't want Papa to find him missing.

He kicked over a gnome on his way to the back gate. Unfortunately, he didn't shatter its ceramic head. All Papa's hatred of lawn decorations leaked out of him and into Sparky each night with the ejaculate. He didn't have enough time to kick them all over and shove plastic flamingos into their orifices if he was to make it back to the shed before suburbia woke.

He stepped into the alley and flashed his fairy lights at the family of rats munching on some rubbish from the local chicken and chips shack. Even the middle classes liked their chicken and chips. They restrained themselves from posting about it on social media. A guilty pleasure, but one to be enjoyed in secret, without the neighbours knowing.

The rats looked at him before returning to suck the marrow out of the bones. He didn't have pockets to hold onto polished decorative garden pebbles to throw at them. If there weren't enough chicken bones out there, they might come for his spunk. It contained a lot of nutrients to keep them going.

The key clanked inside him. He didn't want to swallow down polished stones and accidentally throw the shed key at rodents when he regurgitated the entire mess, lubricated by cum. He needed that jizz to power his circuits.

Karen wouldn't be happy to see Sparky locked out of the shed. An uppity bitch more concerned with the opinions of the neighbours, she'd smash him against the side while Papa looked on, clutching his keytar and begging for mercy.

Next door's shed would be useless to him. Both partners in the couple cried over their failed dreams, but neither had ambitions to be musicians.

One was a wannabe chef who couldn't cook. Sparky sat in the shed and listened to them fight. Plates were smashed by the failed fashion designer, alongside cries of "you gave me food poisoning, you fucking fag."

Sparky wondered if it was okay for gay partners to call each other "fucking fag" in the heat of an argument taking a turn towards violence. He wouldn't normally care, but he had nothing better to do.

Two rows of houses backed onto the alley. Sparky calculated failed musicians in six of them, excluding his own. He resided in a neighbourhood of broken dreams, based on all the shouting happening behind closed doors. If his first expedition produced nothing to give him a voice, he'd start in the alley on the other side of the road in the early hours of tomorrow, after Papa refreshed his spunk supply.

He went into the garden directly behind the house Papa shared with his wife and brats. Even with post-graduate degrees, the children wouldn't ever flee the nest. There's nowhere to go when the older generation own second homes.

The gate wouldn't open. Fairy lights didn't include X-ray vision, but he didn't need it to know the gate was locked and he'd scale the wall. The lock would have been further down the gate, away from his reach. Stretching required more spunk than climbing.

The same cheap plastic flamingos cluttered their garden as well. The pound shop must have them on offer. Three flamingos for one pound. A little bit of instant social climbing in a choice of five garish colours.

They weren't spread out with gnomes. The home owners mustn't have achieved enough status yet to decorate with something other than flamingos. Sparky knew from Matthew's frantic mental shouts during ejaculation that Karen pestered him to move up in the world of voluntary commitments, so she could buy lanterns with little tealight candles in them without prawns through their letter box during their two weeks in Majorca.

Matthew enjoyed better things than teaching snot-nosed brats five-a-side football. Entertainment with charity gigs in a synthpop cover band wasn't worth more than coveted garden lanterns.

Sparky wondered what these people did to have so many flamingos and nothing else. They didn't have a shed. Instead, they were afforded a plastic box.

He looked to the sky. The Moon lowered. He didn't have time to break into the house and find where the residents concealed their dreams. He scaled the fence, leaking cum.

He shoved his finger into his hole. Most of it had been absorbed. Papa's balls were exceptionally heavy. Sparky didn't think he had a chance to wank during his lunch hour. It required too much effort to do it without being caught.

He landed on his tumble-dryer hose legs and clunky old clogs stolen from a charity bin in the local supermarket car park. These people had lanterns and a gazebo. It must have pissed them off, living next to people not willing to give up on their ambitions.

Sparky went in a diagonal line towards the shed, knocking over lawn ornaments on the way. The lock was old and rusty. The home owners had given up on their broken dreams a long time ago, in complete contrast to the people next door. Their flamingos would have stared at them when the residents looked out of an upstairs window.

Sparky didn't know how many gazebos lurked in the neighbourhood, but he didn't imagine it was many. The only thing these residents lacked was a bird bath. They even had an ornamental well, crawling with snails. Pellets weren't allowed in Suburban Hell. There were worse things than prawns to put through letterboxes.

Sparky wished they had the ultimate status symbol. He'd like nothing more than to drop cum nuggets and hide in the shadows as the birds bathed in spunk. Suburbia could become covered in Papa's cum bubbles if Sparky came across one.

He spat into his hand. His plastic head and fairy lights separated pre-ejaculate from the gooey white stuff. What landed in his hand from beneath his bucket head was the pre-ejaculate, perfect for dissolving metal and breaking into garden sheds.

4

Layers of dust greeted him. Too much of it. If it was discovered, the residents would have to knock down their gazebo and forever be banned from owning a bird bath. Sheds were expected to be clean, even if they were never used. It was a matter of safety for the residents of Suburban Hell.

Sparky went back outside and uprooted a chilli plant. He needed something to remove the dust; otherwise, he wouldn't know what objects lived beneath. He flicked the slugs onto the climbing rose bushes, impaling one or two on thrones. He didn't believe slugs ate chillies until about twenty fell from the plant.

Slug-free, he grabbed a plastic flamingo concealed in high, decorative seagrass. These people weren't good enough to do away with them entirely. Anyone in Suburban Hell could plant seagrass. If the flamingos didn't delight Karen so much, she might consider hiding them amongst it.

The stick would shift the cobwebs, so they wouldn't become tangled on his chilli-plant duster. He poked the stick into the shed and swirled it around, using the flamingo as a handle.

The action made him think of the images of candy floss being made that he picked up from the memories in Papa's spunk. This candy floss included offerings of spiders instead of crunchy burnt sugar. If Sparky required food, he would eat it: vengeance against the spiders crawling into his hole every night and eating his creamy insides.

A few more swirls and it weighed down his flamingo stick, making it difficult to keep his vacuum-cleaner arms up. He discarded the stick by the side of the shed.

Most gardens in the neighbourhood would include more plastic flamingos within arm's reach. The occupants of the house it belonged to were clearly special with their variety of lawn ornaments. They might even be junior doctors. They'd perfected wallowing in misery and putting it on display in the garden.

Sparky had to move back a few steps, knocking over a garden lantern to reach another plastic flamingo on a stick with his arms stretched out. It seemed to be of a slightly higher quality than the flamingos Papa saw in his own garden. The residents were playing with fire, though not literally. Literally would be prawn cocktail through their letter box during their summer holidays to Majorca.

He went back to the shed. Fairy lights didn't illuminate much, but he was able to see he could step inside without becoming tangled in cobwebs. He thrust the stick end of the plastic flamingo in. His eyes couldn't penetrate the gloom in the back and surrounding objects, no matter how high he turned up the brightness. A shed in a garden with a gazebo would include a light somewhere beneath the dust.

He pulled away another stick with cobwebs and mummified spiders. This stick reminded him more of papa's hair way back when the keytar was used every night, before the kids were born and Karen cranked her nagging up a notch. Papa still pictured himself with hair teased up with enough hairspray to claim sole responsibility for the hole in the ozone layer.

Liquid leaked from Sparky's eyes. Cum was thicker than water, but he had to be careful not to short-circuit the fairy lights. He threw the stick out of the door. Out of sight, out of mind. That was what Papa thought when he blew his load into Sparky's lined hole, anyways.

He flicked tears of jizz into the shed. They couldn't land with a splat with inches of dust coating every surface. He grabbed the uprooted chilli plant and went to work. More slugs found their way onto it while he was occupied removing cobwebs. He flicked them into the garden.

The occupants weren't afforded enough status to hire a cleaner for their shed. They wouldn't want their dreams from yesteryear put on display for the neighbours. They wouldn't want to be reminded of them, either.

Sparky went in, armed with the chilli plant. Somebody had a secret nicotine addiction they kept alive out in the shed. It was obvious from the way the dust stuck to the objects and the faint smell of stale tobacco curdling his cum.

He rubbed the plant along harder, faster. The interior required sugar soap. Sparky didn't have enough time for cleaning. Baby chillies fell as he unearthed a box, sticky with nicotine. He pulled the box out of the shed, tucking the chilli plant into the bucket handle that served as his mouth.

Sparky pulled the box open to a mummified rat. Papa's spunk told him that shouldn't be possible in a country with so much rain. Sparky pulled it out by the tail and held it to the moonlight. The rodent had long since died. Sparky lacked time to give it an examination if he was to make it back to his shed before Papa and Karen woke.

He threw it towards the centre of the garden. It landed on a gnome's pointy hat. It seemed like the best place for it. Spying on the neighbours brought Karen joy under normal circumstances. She'd cry if she saw a mummified rat impaled on a garden gnome. Gnomes were sacred, unlike happiness.

He dumped out the box. Tubes of oil paint fell out. Even if he wanted a new coat of paint, it wouldn't do him any good. Oil paint took forever to dry. He left the box where it was, topping it up with the chilli plant, and scaled the wall into the next garden.

5

More flamingos littered the grass. Sparky didn't realise the pound shop in the town centre sold so many of them. They must have a special stockroom filled with flamingos to satisfy Suburban Hell's needs.

There was one lonely lantern in a place of pride in the centre of the garden, surrounded by polished stones. One half of the partnership sleeping in the house would have gone down hard. The lantern placement would be a daily reminder of burying their dreams.

Sparky wondered if Karen could see into the gardens from the upper floors of the house. If her nagging wouldn't drive Papa mad, her jealousy would be a funny thing to watch its course run. Purely for science, of course.

Sparky kicked the lantern over and listened for the sound of glass cracking onto polished stones. The only sounds were the rats in the alley and the mating calls of foxes. Sparky backtracked to smash it. The trail would lead back to his shed. Karen would be blamed. She was known throughout the neighbourhood for her jealous streak.

When broken dreams were replaced with lawn decorations in Suburban Hell, women were the ones to carry the weight and climb the social status ladder with the pound shop decorations (and, if they were lucky, hand-painted gnomes from Karen's father-in-law) strapped to their backs. It didn't matter if they were the ones reluctant to give up on their ambitions for a better life, doing what drove the passion through their blood.

Sparky pulled two plastic flamingos from the lawn and waved

them around while dancing on his dryer-hose legs. The only creatures around to watch were the rats. With Papa responsible for his birth, Karen would be blamed no matter how many faded dreams Sparky ripped out of the shed in the night. Divorce would be in the air. Stressful, until Papa realised he was free to keep the keytar out and play whenever he wanted. Sparky danced harder to a synthpop beat ripped from Papa's memories.

Suburban climbers didn't like the neighbours to see they used to dream of being somebody. A sudden breeze blew across Sparky's body, bringing with it yesterday's newspaper. Sparky didn't need to look to know he now wore a dress made from the *Daily Mail*'s front page. There weren't any *Guardian* or *Mirror* readers in Suburban Hell.

Once Sparky had what he needed, he'd continue his raiding, if only to get the suburban families to admit they were going to be different. More sameness with uniform red brick and conservatories in the gardens for those who could no longer remember who they used to be.

He broke into the second shed and looked inside. There wasn't any dust, not even a snowfall of cum like Papa's shed. The sheer number of flamingos told him the residents sleeping in the house it belonged to weren't ready to give up. The poison that carried on the air in Suburban Hell had seeped into their bloodstream, though.

6

Wires and bits of plastic littered the work table. A bag of fertiliser sat on the floor, half-concealing a canister of petrol. It looked more like a bomb-making studio than the failed dreams of a potential inventor, until Sparky saw lights glowing at him and wondered if it could be both.

He went up to the robot and poked it. He wondered if he looked the same. Papa's eyes caught something that looked entirely different when he pumped into him. The robot on the shelf reflected Sparky's flashing eyes. His arms sat behind the same casing as his head and torso. Sparky was made of different parts, purchased or found at different times.

The second robot poked back, right in one of Sparky's eyes. Sparky was built with an entire string of fairy lights in his head. The robot poking him back didn't have fairy light eyes, but laser pens sticking out of his forehead.

Sparky let the robot poke again. If any damage was done, it wouldn't take much effort to change them. The poking robot had fingers covered in the same casing as the rest of him. Envy tinted Sparky's cum green. He was being like Karen! The green turned red with anger.

Two robots in Suburban Hell. There might be more. All of them might be in better shape appearance-wise than Sparky. Sparky took the other robot by the shoulders and shook; it was only a little angry and jealous.

"No."

The other one had a voice. Sparky's eyes would have grown wide, but they were Christmas lights and couldn't. They stopped flashing for a full ten seconds.

"Who are you?"

Sparky shook his head without removing his hands from the other robot's shoulders. He put too much enthusiasm into it, and cum fell out of the holes drilled into the bucket for ears. He couldn't blush, due to being made with plastic and brought to life with love, but his eyes went pink as he shoved fingers into his ear holes.

Confident the spunk would stay inside where it was needed, Sparky moved one hand to his mouth, looked down, let one drop of cum fall from his eyes, and shook his head in a slow and deliberate action. He then pointed in the direction of Papa's shed.

"I'm called Sandy because inside, the man-juice that powers me turns to sand."

Sparky's eyes flashed to indicate understanding.

"Why don't you have a voice?"

Sparky's eyes flashed quickly with anger.

"Oh, right. You can't say. Nothing in this shed will give you one, but if you help me out with some legs, I'll help you. You scratch my back, I scratch yours."

Sparky's eyes travelled down Sandy's body. Wires stuck out from his torso. The robot had a third leg. A crusty old vibrator was secured where a cock would be, but he wouldn't be able to walk on it. Hop, maybe, but Sparky didn't have the voice to express what he needed to say. Sparky pointed to it.

"My Papi harbours fantasies." The way Sandy said it indicated it was a closed topic.

Sparky shook his head and waved his arms. He pointed at the crusty old dildo again while hopping on one leg.

"Over there. Those are my legs."

Sandy pointed. Sparky gave up on his attempts to get Sandy to hop. He turned his bucket head and saw the legs Sandy pointed at, beneath a layer of white dust that could only be dried jizz. Sparky reached for them, curious about the removal of Sandy's legs.

The temperature must've been up, because some of the snow was wet and salty. Sparky didn't have a tongue to stick out and catch the falling flakes. He imagined what the taste would be like. It wouldn't be as nice as Papa's. Sandy's Papi seemed to have a hateful streak, based on the laser pens sticking out of his robot. It would be written into the spunk as extra salt and bitterness.

He held his eyes up. The fairy lights flashed as dried cum landed on them. A wet flake blinded him in one eye.

"Hurry up with my legs."

Sparky grabbed the legs and turned around. A glob of cum dripping from his face reflected the glow of Sandy's eyes.

"If I had a tongue, I'd lick that. Wipe it away."

Sparky obeyed. Instead of flicking perfectly good cum away, he wiped it in the holes that served as his ears and pulled his eyes through at the same time. The more spunk he consumed, the stronger he would become.

Sandy didn't say anything, but the way his eyes looked at Sparky made Sparky's circuits crawl. Sparky was beginning to wonder if his mission was a mistake.

"Hook them up."

Sandy waved his arms at the wires sticking out of his torso. Sparky didn't enjoy being ordered about, but he tolerated it the same way Papa tolerated Karen's incessant nagging.

The top of the legs included matching wires. Sparky would have sighed, but the only sound he could make was the clacking together of the fairy lights inside his head. The keytar, sitting alone in Papa's shed, never seemed so appealing.

It was too late to turn back now and scavenge the parts. Sparky didn't want to hurt Papa. Damage to the keytar would murder his remaining dreams. And with them, Papa's spirit would die, leaving behind a wake of anti-depressants and sad cum.

Sandy's demanding neediness might ruin Sparky's dreams. He only wanted a voice, and to see Papa happy.

Sparky attached Sandy's legs to his torso.

"You need to connect the wires."

Now you tell me, Sparky thought. He couldn't roll his Christmas tree lights. Sandy couldn't roll laser pens, either.

He pulled the legs away and shoved one into Sandy's arms. The seconds ticked by without Sandy taking it. Sparky would have to return to his shed before long.

Sparky pulled it away and hit Sandy over the head.

"What was that for?"

Sparky dropped the other leg, grabbed Sandy's hand and pushed the leg into it. He then clasped Sandy's fingers around it, unsure if Sandy was fucking with him or had some circuits missing. He couldn't grow an extra pair of arms out of his arse to hold a leg while he attached the other.

Sparky wasn't programmed to pick up thoughts. An oversight on Papa's behalf; he could rectify it once Sparky found a voice and requested it.

He stared into Sandy's fancy laser pen eyes for one full minute, trying to work out if the other robot was mean or simply dense. He might as well stare at a brick wall for all the good it did.

He picked the dropped leg off the floor and connected the wires before connecting it to Sandy's torso. Sandy could do it for himself. Even a dense robot with sizzled circuits would be able to figure it out.

It made a grinding noise as Sandy kicked his plastic penis. The dildo was half lit up. LED lights, instead of a laser pen attached to it. Laser pens must tear the anus. Sparky missed Sandy's kicks to his bucket head.

He snatched the other leg out of Sandy's hand and took a step back to glare at Sandy in what he hoped was a menacing way. He couldn't be sure with fairy lights for eyes. He tilted his head down and angled the fairy lights with their tips pointing up.

Standing like that for a minute gave him a chance to reflect on his lack of a cock, and on the hole Papa filled with spunk in the early hours of every morning, except those mornings it splashed wasted all over the keytar. The keytar would never come to life. Lost cum on her turned to dust.

"Hey, robot, put on my other leg."

Sandy could put on his own leg if he really wanted to. Sandy was the type used to someone doing everything for him. That wasn't the way robots were meant to work, unless his maker's secret dream happened to be servitude. Looking around the shed, Sparky didn't think that was the case. How the man eluded the anti-terror squad and fit into suburbia was anyone's guess.

Sparky stepped closer to Sandy. The light shone from his dildo, illuminating the wires and making the task easier. Once connected, the entire plastic penis lit up. Sparky pushed the leg into the torso until he heard a click, and sand moving around in the foot.

Sandy was ready to go, but he sat on the shelf kicking his legs as the minutes ticked by. Sparky started to leave the shed, knocking over a box filled with wires and rags on the way.

"Where do you think you're going?"

Sparky ignored him, but it didn't stop his circuits from getting a bit hot. He heard Sandy jump off the shelf, knocking things over on the way. Sparky didn't bother to turn around to find out if it was accidental. Sandy was a robot he didn't want to be around, even if his plastic cock offered a guiding light for breaking into sheds.

Sandy caught up quickly. Of course he did! When Sparky put his legs on, he was more interested in the wires. He dismissed the wheels on Sandy's feet. Going back through the circuits with the memories, Sandy had roller skates for feet, weighed down with cock-sand for extra balance.

Sandy grabbed Sparky's shoulder and pulled him back. Sparky fell on his arse and spilled cum. Too much lost spunk and he'd be forced to power down without making it back to his shed. Papa wouldn't be allowed to go looking for him.

He stood up and kicked Sandy. Sandy fell. Sparky pulled the dildo from between his legs. Without Sandy's wires, the lights didn't work. Sparky slapped him over the head with his own plastic penis in victory.

He lost some cum with the swing, but not a significant amount. He hit Sandy again. And again. All the rage and anger that built up in Papa's spunk supply came out in those swings. The little bit of Sandy's Papi's jizz he'd sampled only added to the anger. Sparky's circuits buzzed with electricity.

Cum leaked out of Sandy's mouth. Sparky leant down, as if he were kissing the other robot. He wasn't. He sucked up the leaking spunk with his eyes. It didn't hold as much power as Papa's spunk, but it replaced some of what was lost. Sparky didn't want to risk shutting down in the middle of someone else's garden, surrounded by foreign flamingos.

Sandy tried to push him away. Sparky broke off his fingers and hit him with his own plastic penis again. If he had teeth, Sparky would have gnawed on the fingers until they were sufficiently chewed up and spat them in Sandy's face.

He wanted the house owners to wake up to the last of their

shattered dreams scattered around the garden. The robot programmed to carry out destruction with his Papi's spunk, Sparky wanted to pull his legs off again and hang them off the garden decorations. He wouldn't throw handfuls of fertiliser everywhere. It would look less ominous then. He would string up stolen garden lights and put the display of potential explosives in the centre and illuminate it.

The cum inside Sparky boiled. All Papa's disappointments in life rose to the surface, one after the other. They didn't come in clear enough for Sparky to learn what they were before the bubbles burst and sank to the bottom of the spunk, to boil up again with different thoughts.

Sparky didn't try to latch onto any particular thought. He let the emotions course through him. Papa was a man ready to explode with frustration and join Sandy's Papi in his shed constructing homemade bombs. Nothing would make Papa happier than blowing the smiling gnome faces to smithereens. Sparky didn't think that was the sort of explosive destruction Papi had planned, though.

There wasn't a flamingo in reach to beat Sandy with and stabilise Sparky's boiling thoughts. Sparky kicked Sandy. Sandy's hard outer casing put a dent in Sparky's clogs. Sparky didn't mind. He wasn't programmed to feel physical pain, only Papa's mental anguish.

If Sparky didn't damage the wires going into the legs, he could have a new light-up cock and become a real robotic man. He kicked Sandy again. And again.

Each time, with a fresh blow to the head, Sandy buzzed with the circuits misfiring in his body. Sparky liked the sound. He wanted to harness the power, but couldn't without swallowing Sandy's creamy insides.

He settled for jumping up and down on Sandy's head. The outer casing finally started to crack beneath Sparky's feet. Sandy twitched his fingers, only increasing Sparky's desire to bite them off. Once he found a voice, he could request teeth filed down into points.

The circuits to Sandy's arms disconnected beneath Sparky's stamps on his head. The dildo flashed. Sandy's legs still worked.

"Why, Sparky? Why?"

With each stamp and kick, Sparky lost more cum. He bent over and licked Sandy's shattered head. The salty goodness would keep him powered through the night. Some of Papi's thoughts would mix with Papa's. It might offer a way to save the residents of Suburban Hell from themselves.

Plastic flamingos stared at him as ceramic gnomes watched. Their nightly frolics had been interrupted by two robots. Sparky knew they came alive when the residents slept. Cum from Sandy confirmed his suspicions.

Sparky avoided Sandy's legs. Even with the circuits busted, Sparky didn't trust him. Willpower was something that might still exist somewhere in the world. Sparky knew it coursed through Sandy. Papi's spunk told him so.

Sparky reached for the dildo. Without Sandy's wires, it didn't work. Sparky had left his shed for a voice, not a cock.

He wanted a light, though. It would make peeking into the sheds easier. His fairy lights were good enough to bring cheer to a Christmas tree; they weren't good enough to light up the night.

Sparky hit Sandy over the head with the plastic penis one last time and left to scale the wall into the next garden. It didn't seem safe to linger and see if Sandy lied about there being nothing to use as a voice in his shed.

7

Sparky landed in a flower bed in the next garden. He could hear Sandy's howls of "why". He didn't have the time or patience to peel away Sandy's outer casing and find the wires controlling his voice. He should have bashed him over the head one more time. Too late to look back now.

With the wind picking up, Sandy would be mistaken for a sudden gust by the inhabitants of Suburban Hell. A breeze didn't stop Sandy's voice from boiling Sparky's cum. Only silence would do that, and a darkness in Sandy's eyes.

A cat hissed in Sparky's face and took a swipe at his fairy lights with its claws out. Sparky threw the dildo at it. It wasn't any use to him without the light. The cat ran off to fight over chicken bones in the alley.

Clouds drifted over the moon. It didn't matter. The garden had lights leading to the shed along a path of polished pebbles.

Sparky looked around. Only two plastic flamingos. Karen must find it difficult to conceal her hate of these neighbours. Her passion in life involved convincing Papa to sell his keytar so she could buy all the garden decorations to bring envy to the neighbours' hearts.

The garden gnomes were up to something naughty. They weren't the gnomes hand-painted by Matthew's father. Even if Papa's father made these sorts of gnomes, Karen would have forbidden him from supplying these neighbours with any. Obviously, they were much further along in conformity than Matthew was. They were at a place Karen could only dream of reaching.

Gnomes with their trousers around their ankles and cocks in hand, they would have been specially ordered from Etsy. Karen kept special hatred for neighbours allowed to order hand-crafted garden items without half a salmon shoved through the letter box during the dog days.

The people in the house were only a few garden decorations away from the ultimate betrayal of their dreams. It looked like the best garden Suburban Hell had to offer. It would have required extra care and time to maintain such a beautiful place. It even had a little waterfall with Buddha's head sticking out of the side, where the residents could meditate away the emptiness that came with trading their ambitions for gnomes.

Sparky looked at the shed. It looked clean from the outside. The path led to it. It was a path that would only see footsteps to add an extra coat of stain and check the roof.

In gardens with selections of ornaments, the sheds weren't well-kept due to lack of use. The people sleeping away the night without any dreams would have replaced their old broken shed with a new one once they reached a certain level of emptiness. New sheds were only allowed for appearance purposes, once people forgot who they wanted to be.

Sparky looked at the house. The outline of a conservatory stuck out of the end. In the dead of the night, Sparky couldn't tell whether the windows were clean and installed with blinds, but he assumed so in a garden with only two flamingos.

He didn't have time to examine every ornament, but they seemed to all be there, except the ultimate prize: a cherub pissing into a fountain. Sparky couldn't imagine what the middle classes would want with such an object. They weren't even real marble, as he heard Matthew shout at Karen, but plaster.

Papa wouldn't be giving up his keytar for such a vile statement for all the neighbours to see. According to Karen, that was the point.

Sparky banged on his head a few times. He needed to swirl the spunk around to lose the memories and focus on the task at hand. Cum leaked out of his eyes. He wiped it with his fingers and sucked it back in. He couldn't be losing any power and risk not waking.

He went over to the shed. The lock shone at him. Even that looked clean. If he couldn't see the worms squirming beneath the dirt, he would have wondered if the grass beyond the path was artificial.

He heard vacuum cleaners being used outside in his long hours spent in the shed waiting for more juice. Plastic grass didn't signify any additional status for the chattering class. Karen could safely buy some without the unofficial residents' association pouring seafood sticks through the letterbox when they were away for two weeks in mid-July. Papa put his foot down. He wouldn't allow it.

Sparky shook his head. He didn't care about fake grass. He cared about what might be in the shed.

He looked into the keyhole, holding his fairy lights steady. It appeared clean inside. The residents seemed like the sort to have a cleaner pass the duster around inside once per month. That wasn't normally allowed, but exceptions could be made for people willing to put on the appearance of perfection.

Everything was perfect, like their garden. Even their polished stones must get washed every few weeks. Pressure washers would scatter them, so they had to be done by hand. Any self-respecting cleaner or landscape gardener would laugh in the face of someone requesting such a feat, so the residents did it themselves, with their own drool.

Sparky stuck his fingers into the lock and moulded them to turn. It didn't seem like the sort he would need to break. He wouldn't want to ruin the perfect suburban garden with broken metal shards waiting to stab through Crocs.

The door popped open on well-oiled hinges. The lights went on automatically. Sparky wasn't sure if motion-sensor lights were allowed in garden sheds or not. They defeated the objective of keeping one's hobbies and interests locked away in the garden, where they were meant to die covered in dust in the dark.

He went in. It was obvious the cleaning lady came out here frequently, when the other neighbours weren't looking.

Everything of a life that could have been rested in plastic boxes with labels. Knitting items, including a knitting machine, slept on one side, lonely and crying out to be used once again. Knitting needles and wool wouldn't do Sparky any good. He wasn't out for a new jumper.

The shelves on the other side might offer what he was after. The death metal poster hanging in the centre of the shed wasn't something for the neighbours to see. The cleaning lady must've had to sign something to keep their secrets.

Milk crates of old vinyl sat below it. Sparky had a brief scan. The occupants of the house seemed really fond of their death metal. Sparky pictured the knitter of the house sitting on a rocking chair, needles in hand, while Cannibal Corpse screamed in their ears and made the house vibrate.

The death metal wasn't the interesting part, or even both husband and wife once having hobbies and interests and things that made them *them*, instead of one of the dull-eyed, slack-jawed flock.

The guitars mounted from the ceiling on a rack piqued Sparky's interest. He knew the neighbourhood kept at least six failed musicians hidden. He could hear them practicing from time to time. He'd found the second. It was a little mark of achievement in his cum. He wouldn't be able to tell Papa until he had a voice.

Sparky plucked at a string. The guitars were used and loved, but not with spunk. The people sleeping away the night never truly gave up on their dreams, regardless of what the ornaments in their garden declared.

Death metal wouldn't offer him a voice. He backed up and knocked over a box of old cassettes. Even if he had a tape deck, he wasn't about to use one of those to speak. The gore on the covers alone told him they weren't what he was looking for.

8

He left the shed for the next garden, listening to Sandy whine as he scaled over the next fence. The garden he landed in contained extra pound-shop flamingos. He couldn't tell with the moon hiding behind the clouds, but he thought they might be painted different colours.

Only one gnome sat visible in the high grass. It looked like one purchased from the pound shop along with the flamingos. Sheets drooped down from the washing line. The people inside had missed the memo about laundry only being dried inside. They'd find worse than prawns through the letterbox when they arrived back from their annual two weeks in Majorca.

Looking around, Majorca would be too far outside of their status. Caravanning in Wales or Cornwall seemed more appropriate, but for one week only. They hadn't earned that second week yet.

A hedgehog came out of the long grass to cross Sparky's path. Hedgehogs were the sort of wildlife suburbia wanted to attract. They tolerated foxes, but only to impress upon their upper-class superiors that they were one hundred per cent down with fox hunting. But only if the hunt was to come through Suburban Hell.

Sparky didn't want to be around when the neighbours discovered the scruffy garden brought them in. The occupants of the house would be blamed for the rat problem.

Sparky looked at the shed. It wasn't in disrepair like the rest of the garden. A hive sat silent on top of it, the bees sleeping. Bee-keeping was meant for the allotment at the end of the street only. No private bees to be kept in gardens. Any honey had to be shared amongst the neighbours with the best garden decorations.

The people in the house clearly didn't care about the neighbours, or how much sushi ended up falling on their welcome mat while they were away. Sparky went to the shed and banged on the door until the beehive fell. There wasn't much to destroy, but with Papi's cum mixing with Papa's, he had to ruin something. The people sleeping away the night inside, with chamomile tea filling their bladders and backing into their kidneys, would care about their bees.

Sleepy bees came out with their stingers poised. A waste of a sting and a waste of a life. Their venom had no impact upon Sparky. The purpose of the bees became clear when Sparky opened the shed.

The neighbours wouldn't approve of the hobby of the residents inside the house. It was a hobby that refused to die and could prove profitable, if they grew the weed inside the loft as well.

Sparky had stumbled upon the shed of the friendly neighbourhood pot growers. They would have mixed a little herb into their chamomile tea to chase them into deep sleep and away from their neighbours' parcels of decaying fish.

The plant wouldn't help him with a voice. He went inside the shed anyways, to ruin the crop. He threw plants out of the shed. Their containers shattered on the path and released a pungent smell into the air. Sparky couldn't smell it, but his Christmas tree-light eyes saw it as a vomit green cloud, competing with the grass for dominance.

It always reminded Papa of the alley behind the club his band used to play in. A few clubs backed onto that alley. No one knew which one held the pot smokers. Papa's fanbase was more teenage girls who wouldn't be able to identify the smell, and less hippies.

As with every other garden, Sparky didn't bother shutting the door. Everyone's hobbies and broken dreams should be out in the open, so they could judge each other on them. He was certain suburbia could create a hierarchy out of broken dreams.

"Oh, so you wanted to be a musician? Well, the wife wanted to be a sculptor and had dreams of an exhibition in the Tate Modern."

The drug growers would be at the bottom, along with Sandy's maker and his bomb assembly kit. Suburbia wasn't the place for ambitions, unless those ambitions included a better credit rating and car than the people next door. Life goals that bordered on the illegal, or hobbies that were outright against the law, would be frowned upon.

9

Sparky landed on top of a pile of polished pebbles in the next garden. He looked around. LED party lights hung from a wooden structure lining the path. Middle-class suburban people didn't know anything about parties, unless a former DJ lurked amongst them, hidden behind net curtains and a decent car.

Solar-powered lights stuck out of the grass to either side. Karen didn't have those. Matthew's love of the keytar was in the way.

Five flamingos on sticks stared back at him. They didn't look like pound-shop decorations from where he stood, but he couldn't be sure. Sparky wasn't about to examine them.

The shed had been covered with a tarp. That didn't say much for the condition of whatever broken dream waited inside. The people living in the house would need to replace the shed with their shattered dreams inside before they'd be allowed a conservatory.

One of Papa's father's garden gnomes stood guard. Sparky kicked the shed and the entire thing collapsed in a heap of splinters and wet wood. Gnomes weren't good guards. He left the smiling gnome in one piece. He could go tell all his little gnome friends about the shed being kicked to lure them into a false sense of security.

Rats scurried out of the rubble. Suburban Hell residents would scream, but no one had the common sense to phone Environmental Health. Rats weren't a problem in that part of town, they would say, and look in the general direction of where the builders and tile layers lived.

Sparky stared at the pile until an old computer with a shattered screen stared back. He tossed aside a board. Floppy disks gave way to a younger computer. It was a hobby that died a slowed death. A circuit board from a computer might provide a voice, if everything wasn't covered in mould and dust and the dust of ancient mould spores.

The breeze turned the pages of a bright portfolio. Not even dust from a collapsed shed could dull the colours. The person the shed belonged to wanted to work in graphic design. That would have been worth a nice flat in the nice-enough part of the city, with the moderately successful people who decided on temporary poverty instead of Prozac and lawn flamingos.

The confirmation came when a canvas bearing Andy Warhol's face nearly decapitated Sparky. Of all the graphic designers to admire, it had to be the most well-known. It explained why the occupant of the house rested his or her head in Suburban Hell instead of a big city somewhere, working for an advertising firm.

He examined the contents that landed at the top of the rubble enough. He didn't have the time for anymore, especially knowing the equipment wasn't in good condition. He dragged the portfolio to the centre of the garden and ensured it lined up with the kitchen window. Whoever the house belonged to would see it when they put the kettle on.

10

He scaled the wall and landed in a great big pile of steamy dog shit. Big dogs weren't allowed in suburbia. The Staffies and Rotties were for the other side of town. Respectful people required respectful pets. Sparky had trouble believing a Yorkie could create such mess, unless it pooped in the same place every time.

He stepped onto the grass and wiped his feet, happy he didn't have Sandy's wheels. Dog shit would be a chore to get out of those. The residents would end up with fish parcels if they let too much build up in their garden.

Apart from the dog shit, the garden looked like any other. He counted seven flamingos and a gnome in front of each one. The residents liked to get creative with their garden decoration displays.

There were plenty of lanterns with tealights, but no gazebo or bird bath. The dog shit must prevent them. A pooper-scooper might land through their letterbox during their annual two weeks in Majorca, along with a packet of kippers.

Sparky went to the shed, wiping his feet on the grass. They really needed a good wash. He wouldn't mind tracking dog shit all over Suburban Hell, but he needed to return home to his shed and didn't want Papa to be greeted by a bad smell.

The side contained two glass-paned windows. Curtains kept the outside from looking in. Sparky went around to the door and used his fingers to pick the lock. It didn't matter if it broke; he'd leave the door open anyways, so all the neighbours could see the secrets trapped within.

The door popped open, and he was hit in the eye with the pull-cord light string. A disco ball caught the reflection of the bulb and sent mirrored light fragments to illuminate something sparkly.

The windows made sense. Makeup went on better in natural light. There was a lot of makeup. Sparky didn't have names for everything. Karen only wore the basics, and Papa was only one for a little bit of foundation and eyeliner.

A row of wigs sat on a high shelf, with a spider connecting them with her web. Someone had glued eyelashes to the polystyrene heads they rested on. All the wigs were styled and ready for use, if it weren't for the spiders and the hair resting in rat droppings.

A microphone on a stand holding a feather boa gave Sparky a bit of hope. Facial hair bleach on the shelf below the wigs gave Sparky a bit more. The person this shed belonged to wasn't a woman, but a drag artist. If the owner altered his voice, he might have something lying around with his other performance items.

Sparky pulled open an old wardrobe filled with glittery dresses on hangers. He threw the dresses behind him, looking for something, anything that would give him a voice. Dead moths wouldn't work.

The makeup drawers offered nothing except lipstick and foundation with various false eyelashes and products he couldn't name. He grabbed the eyelashes, with some glue, and stuck them to garden decorations on his way to the next shed. He didn't have the time to give the gnomes a full makeover.

11

Sparky scaled the fence and landed in a birdbath. Cum leaked into the water. He hopped out. He couldn't risk losing any valuable spunk. It didn't matter if the thought of Suburban Hell waking up to jizz covering everything was amusing; he needed the power to get back home.

The Moon came out from behind the clouds. He spent a long time scattering dresses, looking for a voice. He'd have to be heading home soon.

"Please, wait."

Sparky whipped his bucket head around and smashed it against the birdbath. Cum went flying.

"I'm injured. Help me."

The cum left inside swirled around. The fence behind the birdbath moved.

"We could be good together."

Sandy.

Sparky backed away from the birdbath with his hands over his eyes, trying to keep the jizz inside. With the spunk settling, he could make out how far away Sandy was. Sandy sounded like he'd made it as far as the graphic designer's garden.

Sound carried weird, distorted by the night. Sparky thought he heard Sandy sifting through the rubble of the shed, looking for a plastic cock, looking for a weapon.

Sparky wouldn't lose his search for a voice. He went to the shed without bothering to take in the garden and see how the neighbours compared to Papa and Karen. He shoved his finger into the lock and pulled the door right off the hinges, throwing it behind him.

He pulled on the light to monitors and recording equipment. He fell forward upon a guide to Britain's ley lines and nearly crashed to the floor. A wall with Aleister Crowley's scowling face painted onto it saved him from losing more cum.

Sparky suspected the monitors and recording equipment weren't normal monitors and recording equipment, even if they only had a sticker with "white noise detector" and a hefty price tag slapped on them to set them apart. A white noise detector picked up sound, it didn't release it.

He had a brief look around. It was possible the shed's owner manufactured their own ghost sounds. Above Aleister Crowley hung a pin board with pictures tacked on. Each picture contained a circle around a fuzzy bit that could have as easily been lens reflection as it could have been a ghost.

The spunk inside told him he wouldn't find what he was looking for. He left, pissed off and empty-handed. He took it out on a garden gnome.

Robots aren't meant to have feelings, but that only applies to normal ones, not robots powered by their Papa's man-juice. Jizz happened to be ripe with intense emotion, due to the moment of ejaculation containing heightened senses.

12

Once the dust of the gnome settled, Sparky caught movement from the fence.

"Wait for me. I want to come along."

Sandy caught up to him.

"I'm powered by cum too. We're two of a kind and none better."

Sparky held out his hand for Sandy to stop approaching. Sandy didn't come across as stable. Whatever spunk ran through his circuits was tainted with the problems of the jizz factory's owner.

Sparky could feel it right down in the wires of his fairy lights. It wasn't a very good position for a robot without a voice to find himself in. Sparky shook his head for no and stopped his fairy lights from flashing in a bid to appear menacing.

"Cut it out. We need each other. I'll help you find a voice and you can help me display the neighbourhood's secret dreams."

It sounded reasonable, but Sparky knew there'd be a catch.

"Me and you, what do you say?"

Sandy clapped him on the shoulder. Sparky backed up, watching the Moon sink lower in the sky. The Earth would turn grey as soon as the Sun started to come up.

Taking Sandy along would waste time. Leaving Sandy behind would waste time and could prove to be violent. He made the motions to indicate he was in a rush.

"I understand."

Less than a second later, Sandy was ripping Aleister Crowley's face apart. He didn't understand. He said one thing and meant the opposite.

13

Sparky scaled the wall into the next garden. He wanted to look around and see what sort of status the house's occupants held in suburbia, but time marched on. He went straight to the shed.

"Hey, wait up. Don't you want to smash some of these monitors?"

Sparky ignored him. Even flipping the bird would take precious time away from him.

He didn't bother with the door and instead charged directly through the wooden boards of the shed, swirling some cum around, but he didn't care. It was too late to care.

Stuffed animals with glass eyes stared back at him. It chilled his creamy insides. Moths fluttered around towards the light, crawling out from the fur and straw. Sparky's Christmas-tree lights weren't as bright as the bulb overhead, but they flew at them too. They hadn't seen artificial light for quite some time, if the dust was anything to go by.

Chicken wire sat in a dusty roll in a corner, covered in spiders. They moved. The budding taxidermist had long since given up on his dreams. Their lives were safe, unless Sparky needed spider guts to compliment the cum and crawl home. Sandy might see them and squish them between his fingers. Sparky wasn't about to waste time protecting the lives of spiders.

Sparky left for the next shed. Someone with dreams of preserving animals wouldn't have anything that could be programmed to use as a voice. He didn't fancy putting glass eyes over his fairy lights.

He needed someone with modern computers, not covered in

dust and mould. Or a musician. Musicians, failed or otherwise, tended to have the best computers, all except Papa.

He kicked a few lanterns over. Papa shouldn't have traded in his dreams for lawn flamingos.

"Hey, can any of this ghost-hunting shit be useful?"

Sparky went into the shed and grabbed a stuffed otter by the tail. He needed something to defend himself with. He missed Sandy's dildo. That thing was good solid plastic. He shoved the stuffed otter into his bucket handle and went for the next fence.

Even if the budding taxidermist of two decades ago inserted sounds into the animals, they would be animal noises. Communicating in growls might be useful for dealing with Sandy, but it wouldn't help him express his ideas.

Sparky needed something like guitar strings and a synthesiser. Papa would be less than pleased if Sparky took apart his secret synthesizer and rebuilt it in his throat. It wouldn't be as painful as using keytar pieces, but he'd still be pretty damn upset. He needed to learn how to make the words that danced around in his head come out of his mouth, once he had the parts and speaker to ensure he was heard.

14

He scaled the fence and dropped into a stinky compost bin. Compost bins were free agents in Suburban Hell, but they were meant to be covered. Residents didn't want to attract the wrong insects. Flies and wasps were unsightly, especially if they became caught in the net curtains for anyone passing by to see.

He knocked over the compost bin climbing out and stepped onto the lid. He threw it like a Frisbee over the fence into the taxidermist's garden. He could only hope he decapitated a gnome, or Sandy. But Sandy hadn't made it that far.

The sounds of Sandy smashing apart stuff that was already smashed reached Sparky's cum- and compost-filled ears. Sandy seemed to have a special hatred reserved for the owners of paranormal hobbies.

He shoved a finger inside his hole to pull the muck out while trying to lose minimal amounts of jizz. All over compost was decidedly worse than stepping in dog shit. He'd shove big steamy turds into his hole to be rid of Sandy, though.

Clouds swallowed the Moon again. Suburban Hell would be waking soon. Some still paid tribute to their secret ambitions. Those ones would be the first to wake, followed by the nurses and supermarket employees. Without the Moon shining on him, he didn't know how much time he had.

The shed wasn't in very good condition, but the residents had garden lights. It made no sense. Their shed had to be in good condition to keep their broken dreams locked inside. Those were the terms and conditions for having garden gnomes.

They might be at the awkward stage where they couldn't balance their overdrafts between accounts, or cash out savings to buy a new one as well as pay for the Prozac prescriptions. They'd be at the stage of internal death, but needing to work some creative finance to buy the new shed to house their broken dreams.

Only residents who kept their dreams alive weren't allowed any garden decorations, except an abundance of cheap plastic flamingos to mark them for their condescending remarks. They weren't even allowed flowers, and especially weren't allowed to grow their own food.

Poor shed maintenance indicated they were dreaming instead of working on making their garden better than the neighbours'. They needed to put in the overtime around volunteer work and balancing their overdrafts to buy a new shed. They were only allowed to stay in disrepair for so long. The state of this one shouted their time was nearly done.

The nearly-collapsed shed's garden had some fancy lawn ornaments, too. The unofficial, unelected residents' board wasn't paying much attention to this end of the street. If Karen were to find out, she'd be devastated. She'd lead the mob with offerings of rotten fish through the letter box.

Sparky went over to the shed and touched it lightly. It didn't fall over, which came as a surprise his creamy innards were just about able to process.

He went to the door. The wood was stronger than it appeared. He put his fingers in the lock. It was the only one to offer some form of resistance. The owners mustn't want sushi thrown into their shed when they were away. The house could be aired out. Sheds were like a hot box in the summer.

He pulled and pushed. It didn't want to move. If the owners couldn't get into the shed, they couldn't very well replace it. The unelected, unofficial residents' association would have made an exception. They were stupid and lacked empathy, but only on the surface, as a display of peacock feathers for the upper middle class they sought to emulate.

The Moon peeked out from behind the springtime clouds, a bit lower in the sky. It would be just Sparky's luck that this shed offered what he was looking for. He wouldn't give up on it.

Sparky shoved his fingers into the lock. A cobweb became caught, but he managed to open it. It was no wonder the occupants of the house used such strong wood. Aliens offered more embarrassment than the ghost hunter a few sheds down the street.

Sparky didn't think the people inside the house even remembered their hobby. Once again, he found himself wiping away the dust with an uprooted plant. He could have used the stuffed otter hanging from his handle, but that was reserved for bashing Sandy over the head.

The plants guarded the space as if they kept bodies out here. In their minds, they might. Little green men preserved in formaldehyde, and greys cut into slices and placed between thin sheets of plastic for further study.

Sparky rescued a book beneath the dust to make Agent Mulder green with jealousy. He wanted to hum the *X-Files* theme to himself, but couldn't without a voice. Sometimes, before Papa could go relieve himself in the shed, he had to wait until the neighbours were asleep. He passed the time with reruns of *The X-Files* and *Buffy the Vampire Slayer*. Sparky had all the episodes impacted upon him with Papa's blown loads.

Alien hunters and conspiracy theorists weren't known to keep devices lying in dust that could produce a voice for a robot. He chucked *Proof of Government Cover-ups, Pilots Tell All* to the side. Sparky didn't care about aliens and government conspiracy.

He threw the plant inside and hopped the fence, trying to stay a few gardens ahead of Sandy. He had no interest in humiliating the residents of the house with the contents of their shed. They wouldn't just lose their standing in Suburban Hell, but in the entire town. The last thing Sparky wanted was a bunch of bricklayers driving up in better cars than the residents of his neighbourhood to laugh at the alien hunters.

15

It hurt to think about what wisdom Sandy was subjected to via cum shot. Sandy might pause by the alien hunter's shed long enough to wonder if he should find a wheelbarrow and lug it all home for his Papi.

Sandy's Papi seemed like the type to be well-versed in government conspiracy theories. Seemed like the type to believe every word of them, too, even the ones that contradicted the other ones.

Papi's spunk would have programmed Sandy to destroy rather than conserve. He would have trouble not blowing up the alien hunter's shed, but Papi would like the evidence. The confusion might blow off Sandy's head instead.

16

The garden was beautiful. Sparky paused to admire it, and the shade of green Karen would turn. She wouldn't be able to see into this one from the upstairs bedroom. The angles were wrong.

Each year brought new garden decorations as Papa died a slow death inside. With each extra decoration, Karen received more party invitations, the types of parties held in back yards in Suburban Hell. Respectable parties. Parties held by gardens such as this. Papa might be dead enough for an invite to this garden's Bank Holiday barbeque.

Karen would vomit on her shoes if she saw it, and blame it on too much gin and sun. Sparky could only look forward to taking Papa's load the night after that happened. Papa would be punished for it with her poison tongue, but the cum these episodes provided kept Sparky amused during the lonely daylight hours, when it was just him and the silent keytar.

A few plastic flamingos hung out by the bins. They were surrounded with lattice and climbing vines. The owners wanted them to be discreet. Something for the barbeque guests to squint their eyes and look for, when they weren't puking on their shoes.

The garden lacked the cherub pissing into a fountain, but everything else was there. The residents might earn the cherub fountain before the spring Bank Holiday. Karen would take it as a personal blow. It wouldn't be; only a celebration of the inhabitant's internal death.

There weren't any gnomes painted by Papa's father. The gnomes in the garden weren't from the pound shop, either. They were made-to-order garden gnomes. They were too good for less sophisticated gnomes, another thing Karen would take personally. She might try to woo them with a hand-painted gift. It wouldn't be personal, though, only something cheerful to ease their passing into the maximum Prozac dosage.

The people asleep in the house must have mastered the art of balance transfers between overdrafts. No one in suburbia had any real income. Nurses, teachers, supermarket workers, and office workers weren't known for their high wages. This street, and all the streets like it, was populated by people with the same job descriptions.

Overtime left only so much space for voluntary community contributions, leading to the garden decorations. Burying one's previous identity gave up time it would have otherwise hogged, for the greater good of Suburban Hell.

Sparky would think it was better on the other side of town, but Papa's spunk said something different. They may have been loud after one cheap pint too many. Not even then could the tile dust and scent of the building site leave them. If they came home smelling of something other than cider and manual labour, their wives grew suspicious.

Despite all of Karen teaching Matthew how to behave, he still had the reek of the council estate in his cum. Bad wallpaper and dishes thrown against walls filled Sparky's head as the sperm with childhood memories fought for dominance.

He headbanged, something Papa witnessed on TV rather than doing himself. The action would have messed up his carefully teased hair to resemble the corpses of ten dead squirrels.

Sparky needed to shake away the childhood memories. They served no purpose, not until he had a voice or fancied a trip to the other side of town. Keytars and silly creative ambitions weren't welcome there, either.

Dreams and aspirations were only for heirs and children, so the lower classes could point and laugh. Only when one of their own overcame the bullying and torment would they claim him or her a local done good. Sensible people gave up to do sensible things, like get wasted on cheap cider and punch a door, or buy garden decorations and become experts at personal finance.

Sparky decided to make the occupants of the house a cherub out of the drum kit he found beneath the dust. He could spare a few minutes to do that much for people that obviously went above and beyond in erasing themselves. It wasn't just one drummer, but two.

Sparky thought the first drum kit wouldn't look out of place in a metal band, but it was hard to tell in the dark beneath the dust. Not even spiders and rats squirmed about in that shed.

He threw it over his shoulder and uncovered a smaller drum with a strap. Maybe the dust had weaved it when the occupants' dreams were first moved into the shed, but Sparky didn't find that likely. He pulled it outside.

He stacked the drums up from largest to smallest next to the bird bath, and spared a little spunk to glue them together. The people in the house needed to remember who they were, and what they'd lost to impress the neighbours.

He listened for Sandy and readjusted his compost-covered stuffed otter. He didn't have much time, so drew a pissing cherub with his finger in the dust. He could have offered his stuffed otter as a substitute, but he needed that.

He ran for the next fence. The shed was right next to it. He landed on top of the roof. It seemed new. The person the shed belonged to hadn't been ready to give up. The sheer number of plastic flamingos staring back at him declared that. They were arranged around a garden gnome.

Sparky scanned the garden from the rooftop. There was only one gnome, painted by Papa's father. It must have been a reward from Karen for putting up the garden shed.

He turned around to check on Sandy's progress and stroke his stuffed otter. The thing began to grow on him.

Without his plastic light-up cock, Sandy didn't have much balance. He seemed pretty good at destroying things. A solid four stars out of five. The fifth could be earned when he regained his balance and became more efficient.

Sandy wouldn't be out of place on the other side of town, the side Karen didn't talk about. They never went to visit Matthew's parents. The parents came to them, or they met in a nice country pub for lunch.

Karen wouldn't be caught dead on that side of town. She only let

Matthew into her knickers all those years ago to please the keytar. She wanted to run her stubby fingers along its neck. He was never one she could bring home to her parents, but once the pregnancy kit declared she was pregnant, she had no choice.

Sparky watched Sandy drag alien hunting books out of the shed and fling them across the lawn, decapitating gnomes. His Papi would be disappointed by the primal need for destruction overruling the logic of how useful the stuff in that particular shed could prove. Sparky didn't like how close Sandy was, even if the other robot was distracted and not aware of the trouble he'd cause his maker's blackened heart.

Sparky jumped off the shed. The door was easy enough to unlock. Someone kept it well-oiled.

Sparky walked into fresh spunk falling from the ceiling. He didn't have a mouth to open. He bent over and let it rain into his hole.

The shed's owner needed to get a film ready for a festival, despite her husband's misgivings. He was busy fucking his secretary, so she had the producer fuck her to liven up the editing. Each scene was cut with her panting into a gag. The gag turned on the producer and stopped her from screaming in a combination of pain and pleasure. Sparky found it beneath the computer and threw it out of the shed. She clearly wasn't happy in her marriage, and neither was her husband.

He didn't want to suck all the cum into his butthole. It would power his circuits for a bit longer and give him a different point of view, but it wasn't worth her husband not finding it.

Two could play at the cheating game. Women were more than subservient social climbers. They had dreams and ambitions too. Nothing of the husband was in the shed. He must have given up long ago to chase more obedient women. The cum mixed with Papa's, taking with it a little bit of vaginal juice and KY Jelly.

He went over to the computer and wondered when she had the electric line run out to the garden without the neighbours noticing. Some of the failed musicians still practiced in the dead of night. They would have noticed. It would save them having to discard batteries without being caught if they cornered the film maker and questioned her, perhaps using the gag as leverage.

Sparky pressed the keys. It wasn't a normal keyboard, but one for film editing. It controlled an expensive machine with even more expensive software.

Papa wanted the same machine, but custom built for music-making, with a music editing keyboard. Apparently there was a difference, but Papa didn't know what that was until he had the opportunity to try it out for himself, when Karen was deep into her abusive bondage books and plastic boyfriend.

He didn't have it in him to offer his butthole to his producer, no matter how much Karen pissed him off. He couldn't snap his fingers and make himself gay for one night only, to secure a record deal and his release from Suburban Hell. Papa thought about it. He thought about it a lot.

The computer screen lit up on the frame the aspiring film maker had left it on. Editor and director in one. The producer and financer thought she was nothing more than a simple slut as he slapped his balls against her arse. It was true art on her computer screen. He didn't appreciate that.

He appreciated ass-to-mouth. She wouldn't turn around to take his dick. She was too engrossed in her work and holding the gag up, so he blew his load all over the ceiling. Next time she required money for some flimsy goal of hers, she could go elsewhere.

Sparky enjoyed learning about other people's lives. He didn't want Sandy to destroy this shed. The woman inside the house still kept her dream fresh, no matter how much cum was dumped in her anus.

Her husband wanted her to give it up and get more garden decorations. He was too busy with the secretary to notice much. The film maker didn't have a name, beyond Simple Slut Number Three-hundred and Sixty. Sparky could roll to the end credits, if she'd tacked them on, but he didn't want to waste time.

Her husband had a name. He picked that up from her vaginal juice that floated to the top of his circuits, weighing less and smelling better than the fresh cum. She might want to get herself tested after her night with the producer and financier.

Gerald. Her husband's name was Gerald. His secretary was Steph. They did it in the marital bed. Simple Slut Number Three-hundred and Sixty didn't care as long as she could make her film in peace out in the garden, listening to the fine sounds of poorly tuned and cared for instruments.

Sparky pulled the keyboard out of the computer. He wasn't sure if it was the same one for music. He didn't care. Papa would be able to use it.

And he might go hunting for the owner. Karen could join Gerald and Steph and make it a threesome while they climbed the social ladder in Suburban Hell. Papa and Simple Slut Number Three-hundred and Sixty's eyes would meet, and it would be love. They could go live in the creative part of town.

Sparky took off his head and shoved the keyboard into his torso, dislodging his stuffed otter. He put his head back on and picked up his otter, stroking compost from its fur. Apart from that, he left the film maker's shed intact.

Sandy would ruin it before long. Sparky wished he wouldn't, but the other robot was bursting with semen imprinted with hatred and the need to destroy.

17

Sparky jumped over the fence. A car caught his silhouette in its headlights as he leaped. There shouldn't be cars out in the early hours of the morning. The nurses' shifts didn't start for another few hours. Holiday season was still a few weeks away. Someone might have a secret hobby they dealt with in a rented space in another town. The residents of Suburban Hell were sneaky and manipulative.

Last house on the row. If he didn't find what he was looking for, he'd have to go back to his garden and admit defeat for the night. He only went through a quarter of the houses that the alley gave access to.

Papa's house sat in the middle of the street. He could stick to his own street tomorrow, instead of going across the alley and seeing the rats, or he could do the rest of the houses on this street. He'd decide tomorrow.

The last house on the terrace always caused jealousy amongst occupants. It had a bigger garden with more decorations. About half of the lawn ornaments were flamingos. The residents mustn't be ready to give up on their dreams just yet.

The stolen keyboard rattled inside Sparky. If Papa had a computer like the one the keyboard belonged to, he'd be able to give Sparky a voice. The keyboard would be a little hint. The rattling told him his cum supplies were starting to shrink. Even if there was another house and the world wasn't threatening to turn grey, he'd have to go home.

Sparky stared at a flamingo. The flamingo stared back. It wasn't plastic. Sparky didn't think that was allowed. He looked at the other garden decorations. They were made of wood, all of them, and painted in bright colours to blend in with the rest of Suburban Hell.

A carved owl looked down from the patio railings. Decorative birds weren't allowed, except for plastic flamingos from the pound shop. Desire to smash it rose inside him, but that would make Karen happy. She was all for sticking to the rules of the neighbourhood.

The world around him turned grey as he stared at the wooden eyes of the owl. Someone had gone to great lengths to carve every feather.

Sparky didn't have much time to look inside the last shed. Based on looking around the garden, he didn't think it would contain a voice. There were a few polished stones dumped by a few flamingos.

Even in the grey light, Sparky could see they were different from the other flamingos decorating the garden. Poorly-painted plastic eyes stared back at him. The paint on their wings ran onto their bodies. The colours were off and neon, declaring they were purchased from the pound shop. The residents of the house, or at least one of them, tried to fit into the social order.

Dirt speckled the pound-shop flamingos. Sparky couldn't be sure in the grey light, but he thought the polished stones lost their gleam. The home owner obviously didn't care for them in the way he or she cared for the wooden ones.

The end house would receive a special sushi delivery every day the occupants were in Majorca or Cornwall, regardless of how well they fitted into Suburban Hell in all the other, more subtle ways. Their garden decorations declared they wanted to be better than their neighbours. Suburban Hell had that in common with what they perceived to be the wrong side of town, with the bricklayers and factory workers.

Karen would suggest they put flaming bags of dog shit on their door step if she spied the wooden ornaments out of the binoculars she kept in her son's bedroom, beneath his used Kleenex. No one else had wooden decorations. Sparky could only guess she hadn't, otherwise the information would have flooded his circuits whenever Papa blew his load. The people inside should be grateful the angle was wrong for Karen's spying.

He went to the shed, listening to the sounds of Sandy a few gardens over. Suburbia would be waking soon to go to their jobs that paid less than the tilers and roofers they looked down upon. The tilers and roofers had an extra hour or two of sleep as well.

The shed in the garden with all the wooden decorations had been constructed by hand. Sparky could tell. It was of superior quality to every other one he'd broken into.

A little workshop greeted him. The people in the house must have thought they were Santa's garden decoration elves. They could have tried giving them away or selling them, but Suburban Hell residents would be too jealous to accept. Talent wasn't something the middle class were fond of, especially if it ran deep and was honed to perfection over the course of many years.

Toys lined the shelves. They couldn't get rid of them fast enough. A bag sat in the corner, overflowing with handmade wooden toys. On the table sat some wrapped in bubble wrap and ready to be put in boxes. Sparky thought they might have a little secret business, which would mean the occupants in the house never gave up.

They worked as a team. Two chairs meant both were at it. If they weren't early risers, everything they made would be smashed. The perpetrators of the crime would never be found. Besides, the police didn't want to arrest middle-aged people with rolling pins for weapons. They had hardened criminals to catch, and drug dealers.

Cum leaked from Sparky's eyes. The keyboard rattled with each passing cum drop. He couldn't help it, though. Papa programmed emotions into him with his spunk.

He shut the door as quietly as he could. He went over the back wall into the alley, landing on a rat.

18

Suburban Hell residents didn't like orange lights shining into their bedrooms. They claimed they didn't have any need for them. Like respectable people, they used their front doors if they were out past sunset.

Only bins lived in alleys. The residents turned a blind eye to the rat population, and managed to pretend the traps baited with poison didn't exist.

No nappies could be found in the alley with the other rubbish, not even the adult kind. The population of Suburban Hell was beyond their baby-producing years, but not yet at the point where they shat themselves.

Sparky pulled the rat from the bottom of his foot by the tail. It was only a young one. He flung it over the wall and into the garden of the toy makers. He couldn't allow them not to receive any sort of damage. The neighbours would suspect their least favourite neighbour of causing the destruction, but the trail would lead back to Papa's shed.

Sparky tried to walk quietly so Sandy wouldn't know where he was. He wanted to make it back to his shed before daylight. Already, lights shone from kitchens and bathrooms with the residents on early shifts.

Despite Karen's continuous nagging about improvement and moving up in the world, Papa didn't do so badly for himself at the office. He was miserable. Everyone in Suburban Hell was. But in terms of having a savings account, he was better than most of the neighbours.

The neighbours couldn't see the savings account. They only saw the volunteer work, leading to approval and better garden decorations. The savings account wasn't any good to Papa unless Karen said he could invest in a home recording studio for the shed. He'd make back the drain by charging the other failed musicians in Suburban Hell for using it.

Sparky counted the back gates as he walked along the alley, trying to dodge rats. Residue in Papa's spunk told him how Karen whispered in her sleep about dressing them up as hedgehogs. The council didn't want to act on them.

Most employees at the offices that fielded the complaints lived on the other side of town, where rats were the least of their worries. Suburban Hell residents reminded them whenever they phoned or stopped in to complain of the rats. They were only one complaint away from moving back to the council estate from which they came.

Sparky paused to listen to Sandy destroy someone's secret hobby and failed dreams. The electric hum from the other robot was enough to make Sparky's cum tingle.

He moved on. The grey light hadn't hit the alley yet. For all he knew, it would be cast in shadow for most of the day. He couldn't read it in Papa's cum because he spent his days at the office.

His Christmas lights flashed, illuminating the way. They caught on the rats' beady eyes and reflected white light back at him. If Papa were to unscrew Sparky's head and drink his spunk, he would learn about the rats in the alley and all Sparky saw in the other gardens. If he hawked it up into Karen's mouth, she'd remain oblivious but have a mouthful of stale cum which, in itself, would be rather amusing.

Sparky climbed the gate into his garden. He dislodged his bucket head for access to his throat. His otter stayed in the handle while he stuck his hand down and pulled out the keyboard. The key for his shed was at the very bottom. He had to extend his arm to reach it.

Papa and Karen weren't awake yet. He'd never seen the inside of the house for himself. Karen wouldn't speak to Papa for weeks, and would force him to sleep on the sofa if she found out he'd constructed a robot in the shed when he should have been planning for volunteer five-a-side children's football coaching.

Sparky checked the shed. He wanted to make sure Sandy wasn't waiting for him in the shadows. All had been quiet as Sparky walked through the alley. With Sandy nowhere to be seen or heard, Sparky locked himself in.

If Sandy was in there, the door would be damaged. Sparky couldn't help but proceed with caution. He still didn't have a voice, and would therefore need to go out again after Papa fueled him up.

Sparky hopped onto the table and glared at the keytar before shutting down for the day. He woke to a banging, his circuits taking a few seconds to fire up due to lack of jizz. His eyes twinkled on.

"Hey, you, why'd you go away? Come out. We aren't done."

Sparky would have laughed if he had a voice. Sandy sounded like he was trying to be intimidating, but the words sounded silly in the robotic voice.

"Oi, damn hooligans! What's going on out there?"

Sparky heard Karen yelling, and her footsteps coming down the path. It sounded like she was wearing her Crocs. She would make fun of Papa for his hair looking like ten squirrels died on his head way back in the 80s when bad fashion choices were all the rage, yet she wore those things. If Papa wasn't so used to Karen's snide remarks and bad choices of her own, it would have blown Sparky's circuits.

He hoped she'd trip over a gnome. That was what should happen to people in Crocs, but in a way so its pointy ceramic hat ended up violating her anus.

"Fuck!"

Sparky thought the voice came from a few gardens away. Karen screamed. Sandy hissed. Sparky didn't realise the other robot could do that. He wondered if he'd be able to do it himself when he found a voice.

"Matthew! This is your fault. I told you to get rid of it."

Sparky knew Karen had no idea about his existence. Sheds were only for residents who kept a dirty little secret of their past they refused to let go. Everyone had one. Karen never stepped foot inside.

"Matthew, get out here."

"What's going on out there?"

Sparky enjoyed the pseudo-posh accent of the neighbour. Karen had yet to master it.

"Some of us need our beauty sleep!"

Sparky hoped the owner of that voice didn't have his partner's frying pans. They were cast iron, if their arguments were to be believed. He didn't want anyone to die. He only wanted a voice.

A scream from down the street and across the alley further chilled the springtime morning.

"My shed! My life's work. I didn't want it in the garden!"

He didn't know which neighbour it was.

"Karen, what's going on out there?"

"Karen, what's going on out there," Sandy mimicked.

Sparky couldn't see outside. He imagined Sandy getting closer to Karen. She screamed.

"Get away from me."

She screamed again. Sandy had been equipped with a dildo until Sparky ripped it away. It was the first time Sparky found himself wishing Sandy still had it. Karen deserved everything given to her. Seeing a plastic penis out in the open would offend her to the point her head might explode.

Papa would be a lot better off if he didn't have to bend to her whims. He would have been a pop star. He would have been big. His house would have sat with all the other houses belonging to new money, with a flash car in the drive.

A landscaper would have dealt with the lawn decorations. Sparky read it all in Matthew's spunk, secreted with trace doses of anti-depressants. He needed more than that, or a stronger dosage to deal with Karen.

"What the fuck are you?"

Sparky heard a gasp. Karen must think swear words but never say them, because that wasn't being respectable.

"Karen! That was naughty."

"Help me."

"No can do. He's about to throw his frying pans at me again. It isn't my fault his cooking gives me the runs."

"What's wrong, Karen?"

Karen squeaked.

"Matthew."

"What happened to my shed?"

"What happened to my garden decorations? I worked hard for those."

"I told you to get rid of the ghost-hunting equipment, Sharon."

Sparky heard a slap. Suburban Hell woke to more violence than it had ever experienced.

"Matthew! Where are you?"

Sparky didn't understand why Karen simply didn't go into the house and shut the door. He wanted to see what was going on out there. He could guess, based on the squeals and screams of the neighbours, but he really wanted to know what Sandy was doing to Karen.

He hopped off the table and went to the door. He lay down on his front and pressed his eyes to the crack between the door and its frame.

Red lasers shot from Sandy's fingers. Sparky didn't think they'd do any damage unless pointed directly at Karen's eyes. She froze. The look of horror on her face said all her fears of discovery came true.

Matthew's shed sat in the garden, unopened. Sparky could turn around and watch the dust fall on the keytar. Red lights lit up on Karen's shins. Sandy made mechanical shooting sounds.

"Matthew!"

Urine dripped down her leg. If the neighbours saw, they'd take away her plastic flamingos. The neighbours woke up to their own problems. Sparky couldn't rely upon them to notice her.

He didn't want to open Papa's shed to Sandy. Karen losing her flamingos would make Papa's life harder. Discovery of the keytar would destroy what little spirit Papa had left.

According to the residue in Papa's spunk, he was fully Google searchable. A younger Matthew appeared on the first page of results, hair teased up with a comb and hairspray, keytar strapped around him. The neighbours mustn't be very good at spying on each other. They would have confronted Karen with Papa's dirty little secret.

"Why do you keep us locked in sheds?"

The lasers shone up her legs. Eight of them. Sandy's thumbs pointed at the garden path. No steam or smoke rose from where the lasers pointed at the ground.

If Sparky was out there, his fairy lights would illuminate the wet patch spreading across her nightie for the neighbours to see. He didn't have a voice to hoot and howl and compete with Suburban Hell to draw attention to the situation.

He watched. He waited. He listened.

"What's going on out there?"

The cum powering Sparky tingled at the sound of Matthew's voice. The little extra electricity wouldn't give him a voice. He couldn't hear Papa's footsteps above all the shouting, but he could feel them vibrating through his body. His fuck-cup warmed up, waiting for Papa's cock. It had done that the other day too, while Papa assembled the new barbeque ready for the summer.

Karen was told by the neighbourhood association she was allowed the same model as last year. Papa had a plate thrown at his head. She missed, and it shattered against the wall.

Sparky wanted to throw plates at her head. Processing the red flashing lights not destroying anything took a lot out of Sparky. Sleep wanted to overcome him.

He had to drag himself out of the way of the door. Papa would crush him and scrape him against the floor if he tried to enter with Sparky spying. He pulled himself to the corner and made a pillow out of dried semen and spider eggs. Spiders grew fat in Papa's shed, feasting on all the cum. It contained more calories than flies.

19

"**S**parky?"

Sparky tried to lift his head at the sound of Papa's voice. All he could manage was a flash of his eyes. Papa's balls had ripped another pair of y-fronts.

"Sparky? Where are you?"

Papa grabbed his balls and knelt to look below the table. He didn't even bother to brush his fingers along the keytar.

Sparky's eyes flashed. He couldn't hold them steady without more cum. The flashing might get Papa's attention. To Sparky's circuits, it was like fireworks going off. He knew what Papa would see would be dull and out of the corner of his eye at best, like a five-pence piece dropped in a puddle.

Sparky tried to tap his fingers on the floor. He couldn't muster the power. He needed more spunk. Papa's balls were so full, they bulged out of his hands. He'd get splinters in them if they managed to escape.

"There you are."

The relief in his voice was clear. Papa couldn't reach Sparky without standing up first. Crawling would put too much strain on his balls. His back creaking echoed off the walls of the enclosed space.

Sparky felt one warm hand pick him up; Papa needed the other to keep his balls from dropping below his knees. Sparky didn't have any power left to heat his fuck cup. Papa placed him on the table, grabbed his handle and went in cold.

Sparky felt Papa shiver against him. His otter hit against his head with the motion.

Papa shuddered as his balls released the first lot of cum. Once inside Sparky, even battling the cold, Papa couldn't keep his seed inside any longer than five seconds. One thrust was all it took for the first explosion.

Sparky received the full force of what transpired in suburbia. It would take hours to process it. He wouldn't wear himself down once Papa went back to bed, so he could sift through everything and sort out anything relevant.

While Papa thrust himself in and out, releasing more creamy ejaculate, Sparky searched through the information, looking for anything that was useful to finding a voice. The keyboard was in the shed somewhere, covered in dried cum-flakes. That would be the biggest hint. Sparky grabbed his moth-eaten otter to stop it from falling out of the handle. He didn't want that to land in a pile of dust.

"Sparky? Ha! What a stupid name. You're a girl robot. You should have a girl's name."

"Huh? Who said that?"

Papa's balls seized. Sparky felt them tightening against his plastic. He didn't feel like a girl.

Papa pulled his dick out of Sparky's backside. His balls were bloated. They'd need more relieving.

"Coming out? You still need a voice. We caused quite the bit of chaos last night."

Sandy chuckled from beyond the shed. Papa opened the door. He didn't bother putting his torn underpants back on.

"Well, hello there."

"Hello."

"Come on in. I have some questions for you."

Papa held his dick in his hands.

"Why, thank you sir. But tell me, why did you name your robot Sparky?"

"I don't know. What's your name, little robot?"

"Sandy. Tell me, why doesn't Sparky have a voice? He couldn't tell me what he wanted last night without doing a dance."

Sparky looked at Sandy. Life might get simpler with him on board. Sandy found the keyboard and handed it to Papa.

"What's this?"

"What does it look like?"

"An expensive keyboard you swiped from someone's shed. I look at similar ones on the internet sometimes. One day, Karen will let me buy a new computer for my own home recording studio."

"No one cares about your marital problems. Sparky swiped it, that's the important thing. A little hint, I believe. He should have swiped this from the ghost hunter's shed. At least it has letters on it."

Sandy pulled a Ouija board out of his backside and handed it to Papa.

"Now Sparky can spell out what she wants, or I can simply say it. Give her a voice."

The chaos of garden sheds, torn open for all to see the broken dreams contained within, wouldn't continue into a second night if Sparky had a voice, unless Sandy went on a rampage. He wouldn't be doing it with Sparky, though. Sparky would be able to tell him no.

"I don't have the right parts, Sandy. I answered your question, so you answer mine. What did you two robots get up to last night?"

"Well, sir, Sparky stole my plastic light-up cock and threw it away. I need one of your wife's vibrators to function."

"Nah, you don't want one of them. Her vagina is a lethal breeding ground of menopausal disease."

"But, sir, I need a cock to light my way."

"Why does your way need to be lit?"

"I need to see what dreams people left behind for the sake of garden decorations."

Sparky thought Sandy was picking up on his thoughts and plans for the early hours. As if to confirm it, Sandy turned to look at him. One of Sandy's eyes went out in a strange mimic of a human's wink. Sandy's eye turned back on.

He turned back to Matthew.

"Sparky needs a voice. He's the brains of this operation."

Papa choked. His balls convulsed and a little bit of cum fell to the floor. Sparky needed that cum to finish powering up. The floor would only waste it.

"Sparky . . . Sparky can't be the brains of anything. He's nothing more than a release for me."

"Sparky is a girl. You didn't equip him with a cock."

A drop of cum fell from Sparky's eye. He was a boy. He didn't need a cock. A fuck-cup anus was enough.

"I wasn't about to use one of my wife's vibrators."

"So get one in the pound shop. They sell them."

Sandy's eyes flashed, the closest he could get to rolling them.

"Hurry up with him. Big plans for tonight."

"I can't do it with anyone watching."

"I'm a fucking robot. I have no sentience."

Sandy went to stare into the corner. Spent semen dust snowed upon him. Sparky listened to him huff while Papa watched.

Papa still maintained his erection. His balls started to droop lower. They were clearly heavy. He would need to relieve them.

"Quickly, then, we don't have all night."

Sandy's voice echoed off the wall, dislodging white dust.

"You two shouldn't be exposing everyone's aspirations to the world. There are reasons suburbia keeps its secrets in sheds."

"Don't forget to take your Prozac in the morning." Sandy had no control over the tones of his mechanical voice. He said it the same way he told Papa he didn't have all night.

Papa sighed and turned to Sparky as if it were the most normal thing in the world to be carrying on a conversation about the inner workings of Suburban Hell with a monotonal robot powered by cum.

"Hey, leave some spunk for me, I haven't been home yet."

"Eat dust."

Sparky had never heard Papa speak like that before. Retorts were saved in his head for Karen. He never used them against her, though. She was at the end of her tether, and ready to stab him with the pointy end of a lawn flamingo.

Papa picked up Sparky and parked him on his dick. Sandy mimicked the moaning in his mechanical voice.

It didn't stop the sweat from Papa dripping onto Sparky. Sweat didn't supply Sparky's circuits with power. Only cum did that.

Papa's balls hit Sparky's backside. He held tight to his otter. He caught Sandy watching and snorting spunk-dust from the floor.

Sparky's eyes flashed and lit up the shed when Papa blew his load.

"Save some of that for me."

Sandy stood below Papa and Sparky, red eyes flashing and trying to take in fallen cum-drops. Papa wiped the jizz falling out of Sparky's overfull backside into Sandy's hole. Sandy made a mechanical purring sound.

"That's the stuff."

"You must've contained some reserves somewhere. You were up and moving around. Sparky couldn't lift his head."

Papa picked Sandy up and put him next to Sparky.

"Let's have a look at you two."

Papa scratched his balls as they shrank back down to normal size.

"Why are you digging through people's hidden dreams?"

"I've already told you, Sparky needs a voice. You didn't give her one."

"That's no reason to humiliate people and destroy their dreams in the process."

"Why don't you come with us?"

Papa's face fell. He clearly wanted to join them. Arguing with a robot programmed to be smarter than him, he'd need a good reason not to join them.

"Karen will kill me."

"You're already dead. Inside. Where it counts. She murdered your dreams long ago," Sandy said.

Papa grabbed his keytar and pressed the buttons.

"I can still play," Papa said.

"Silently. In your head," Sandy said.

Sparky wanted to laugh. He couldn't without a voice. His lights flashed instead.

"Quiet, you," Papa said.

"Sparky isn't talking. His lights are flashing," Sandy said.

"He's laughing inside," Papa said.

"That may be true, but you can't build a robot, jizz in your feelings, and then not give her a voice," Sandy said.

"Sparky's a him," Papa said.

"Stop arguing. Come with us. You had dreams once. That much is obvious from looking around your shed," Sandy said.

Papa pressed the keys on the keytar; cum-dust shot up and resettled on the floor. A tear fell from his eye. The world slowed down. The tear tracked through the dust and caught light from

Sparky's eyes, creating a rainbow on its way to the floor. The world still contained beauty, but not much.

Sparky knew what Papa was thinking. It was written in his last semen sample. His keytar would be safe as long as Sparky was around. Sparky couldn't guarantee his secret would be. It wasn't really a secret.

Most of suburbia knew Papa had played the keytar in a synthpop band long ago, much to Karen's humiliation. Much like other failed musicians hidden in the neighbourhood. Their successful counterparts were either very rich and in the gated community, or very poor, surviving from gig to gig and trying to make merchandise popular with the masses on the other side of town, the drive keeping them away from the bricklayers and roofers down at the pub unless they were performing. Creatives didn't need lectures about being uppity snobs too good for anyone else. Papa would rather live amongst them than the residents of Suburban Hell.

"I can't join you. I can't support this. I just can't."

Papa sobbed as his balls refilled. He held his cock in his hand. Sparky didn't think Papa realised he was jerking off. Sparky knew he took his otter out of his handle and stroked it in the same way Papa stroked his cock.

Sandy stood below Papa, absorbing stray bits of pre-cum. Sparky had the good stuff. Papa cried and jerked off and played his silent keytar. It made Sparky's creamy insides sad.

20

He hopped off the table and went out the door. If all of suburbia's secrets were uncovered, Papa could be happy. It was about more than getting a voice.

Sparky scaled the backwall and jumped into the alley. More rats lurked about, dislodged from the sheds. He went in the opposite direction.

Fashion and bad cooking wouldn't help him. Those in the neighbourhood that missed the token gay couple's arguments needed to see what they were about. He went into their shed and dragged their things outside.

He set off earlier than the night before. Papa had discovered Sandy, which led him to Sparky, which meant Sparky could come and go as he pleased, as long as it was in the cover of night.

Sparky stabbed a gnome in the eye with fabric scissors and dressed its nearest neighbour in corduroy. Each one was given a cast iron pan before Sparky moved onto the next garden.

The wall and angle of Karen's viewing window would have sheltered her from the naughty gnomes. The woman's jealousy would end up killing her in the end. Sparky didn't know how. That part wasn't written in Papa's DNA.

He dragged the gnomes to the centre of the garden and arranged them around the birdbath, where Karen was sure to see. He strung garden lights around them, in case she woke up in the night to view the destruction and uncovering of suburbia first-hand by peering over back gates.

He pulled open the shed door to another failed musician. A bass guitar hung from the ceiling, covered in dust and spider webs. Tab books sat in the corner, opposite an amp. Sparky pulled the cables, and out came a selection of effects pedals from the darkness.

Sparky arranged them with the naughty gnomes and garden lights. He stood back and looked. He hoped it was too pretty for Sandy to ruin.

He landed on a pile of polished stones in the next garden. A big pile. There wasn't any grass, but a yard of dirt. At the far corner, just in front of the wheelie bins, sat the shed. Not even people re-doing their garden could escape the shed. It looked new.

The objects it kept secret would have been kept in a plastic garden box not long ago. People with dreams so faded their sheds needed replacing had pristine gardens with lots of ornaments.

Sparky tripped over a plastic flamingo lying on its side in the mud. He lost a little cum. If he needed to go back for more, he was certain Papa would oblige.

He could still hear Papa jerking off in his own shed. Sandy would be filled with extra energy. Sparky didn't view this as a good thing, but Papa's curiosity was written into the sperm, even if it appeared suddenly.

Last night, he'd been nearly spent. The new spunk had dominance in his mechanical body. Curiosity would win the race.

Papa went to work and jerked off into a urinal. All the cum that built up during the day was from after the neighbourhood woke up to their secrets on display. Papa wanted to know everyone's hidden ambitions. He wanted to know which one of each partnership sent the dreams to live in the shed, all for the sake of a few cheap garden decorations.

Sparky pushed himself out of the mud. He left tracks behind. The residents would know the destruction was caused by a robot, if they kept a hidden reserve of common sense and deduction skills. Sparky didn't know how likely that was.

They held onto their ambitions in back gardens, covered in dust. But still, they held on. Common sense was something that had to go for the best garden decorations. If Papa's nocturnal fantasies were anything to go by, they dreamt of a different world, one where they met with success and encouragement. Common sense was outright encouraged in that world, instead of bullied out and replaced with a plastic flamingo.

Sparky opened the shed. He expected it to be empty, and was

most pleasantly surprised to discover it wasn't. It didn't contain a voice, but it contained little speakers he would need to talk.

He swallowed them. He heard a little splash where it landed in cum. He swallowed an extra. Sandy was the type of robot Sparky would need to speak above to be heard.

Sparky dug through the wires and various electronic bits on the floor. The shed was so new, his spunk smelt the pine. It was a scent Papa got off on. Sparky had no way to relieve the feelings that coursed through him. He couldn't even stroke his otter. He'd left that back on the table in his own shed.

The owner hadn't bothered to put up shelves yet. In their mind, it might have been a temporary solution to keep the other half happy. Singletons weren't welcome in Suburban Hell, even if they were well-to-do. Having a partner kept hopes and dreams in check.

Sparky grabbed a handful of wires and swallowed them. He might need them to hook up the speakers. He threw everything else out into the mud and dirt.

The next garden didn't offer a smooth landing. Sparky became tangled in the garden lights falling off the fence. He hadn't seen them because they weren't switched on. They were the string type that needed to be plugged into the mains.

To untangle himself, he followed the rope of lights towards the house. The residents had a plug installed outside. Karen's eyes would bulge out of her head and melt if she knew. They didn't have a conservatory, or naughty gnomes.

That wouldn't matter to Karen. The grass was always greener if someone had something better than her. The expense of running that extra plug would never cross her mind, only why she didn't have an outside plug.

She didn't have anything to plug into it. Papa was granted a petrol-powered lawn mower two summers ago when he rescued the neighbour's cat from a tree. Until then, he'd had to trail the extension cord out of the kitchen window and knock Karen's plants into the sink.

Sparky pulled the lights out. Even if he had lasers, they'd be about as much use as Sandy's to untangle himself. Sparky pulled at the string of lights. They weren't that much different from the fairy lights that lit up and flashed for his eyes. They were so colourful, though.

Every move he made, he seemed to become more tangled. He cartwheeled until they stopped dragging and wrapped them around himself, so his movement wasn't hindered. On his search for a voice, he might find something to turn them on.

He didn't fancy installing solar tiles on his head. Those were popular in Suburban Hell. It gave them something to turn their noses up at the other side of town without realizing the other side of town had installed solar power years ago. They had all the electricians.

And their solar tiles weren't big bulky panels like in Suburban Hell. Papa looked at them with the same envy his wife had for the neighbour's garden decorations. Solar tiles had practical uses, unlike ceramic gnomes.

Sparky kicked the ornamental well in a sudden flash of rage. Papa's paperwork wasn't in order before he left the office. He had to stay behind for an extra half an hour. Sparky took it out on the well and the staring garden gnomes.

He found himself much calmer in front of the shed. He shoved his fingers into the lock in a gesture he'd repeated so many times in the past twenty hours.

The door swung open to a cloud of dust. He grabbed a flamingo and plant and shoved them inside. He discarded them when they became too dirty.

There weren't many flamingos in the garden, but a little flock poked out of the ground by the bins. They didn't even have a flowerbed to occupy. The resident's shame wasn't allowed to be hidden away entirely in the shed. The flamingos were a plastic reminder in bright pink that one of the partnership wasn't ready to give up on life.

The door creaked on rusty hinges. It was a shed that hadn't been opened in a very long time. Sparky went inside. Glass eyes stared at him from porcelain faces. Moth-eaten lace hung down.

He kicked a box. The cardboard fell open with the blow. Pictures tumbled out. He grabbed one. Someone had a morbid fascination. The subject of the picture was dead. Papa had watched a documentary about Victorian death practices not long ago.

Sparky went deeper into the shed. He knew there wouldn't be anything in here to help him speak, but he was curious. Death obsession was something that rubbed off on Papa. A lot of his songs had undertones of death in them.

An old dress hung down from the back like a ghost. Sparky pulled at it. The fabric was high-quality. He took it out of the shed and dressed the birdbath in it. Something so old and pretty should be on display in a museum, but it wasn't in good condition. The birdbath would have to do.

Sparky turned away from the shed and into the next garden with a twinge of regret. There would be time to catch up on Victorian death practices once he found a voice and could better express himself.

He landed next to a lantern. They sat in pairs, all around an outer border of polished stones. Flamingos stuck up on either side of the lanterns, with a gnome standing in front of each display.

The shed sat right in the centre of the garden, in a place of honour to make Sparky's creamy insides boil. Sheds were meant to be sources of shame in Suburban Hell. This one had windows. It wasn't a shed at all, but a little house.

Sparky peeked in, adding power to his fairy lights. He couldn't see much, even though the curtains were open. He went to the door. The lock popped open with his touch. The shed was warm, and not four simple wooden walls. Someone had plastered inside.

Sparky found a switch. It controlled lights. Sketchbooks lined the walls. Pencils rolled around on a table. The dust on the floor wasn't dust, but pencil shavings and pieces of rubber covered in graphite and lead.

Artists didn't provide guitar strings or synthesiser pieces or anything to help him speak, but the owner of the little garden house didn't deserve to have their drawing supplies strewn across their lawn. Sparky found one of their drawings instead and some pins. He pinned it outside of the house.

Papa knew music. He didn't know art. Not much in the spunk could tell Sparky whether it was a good drawing or not.

Sandy would come along before long and tear apart the contents of the shed. If Sparky could preserve the one drawing, things in Suburban Hell might be different. Talent still lurked behind the garden decorations, and a secret determination played out in the sheds.

Sparky hopped over the fence and into the next garden, smashing apart a hedgehog hut. There weren't any hedgehogs inside. They would have torn his new decorative lights. Flowers rose up from beds as tall as him.

A broken garden gnome, like the ones Karen proudly displayed, poked out of the dirt in ceramic pieces. Karen would suffer an instant death if she saw it lying there, covered in mud, colours faded from the shattered pieces.

Sparky stepped over a boundary made of large stones and Buddha statues to enter the path of polished stones. Flamingos lurked in the tall flowers. Sparky didn't think there were many. It was obvious the residents didn't want to look at them while they sat in their conservatory. The reminder of not giving up entirely on their dreams would have taunted them in gaudy plastic every time they looked out to admire their hard work into conformity.

The path of polished stones led around the ornamental well and birdbath. Sparky kicked the birdbath. No one should replace dreams with plaster. It wasn't plaster, but solid rock.

He chipped his plastic foot and wanted to scream. Cum boiling didn't have the same audio impact as robotic cries. Sparky could hardly hear himself bubble, let alone wake up suburbia with howls.

He needed silver tape for the foot. Papa never knew if it was Duck Tape or Duct Tape. He never needed to use it.

Solid birdbaths were intended only for the elite. The people sleeping in the house were batting too far ahead of their station, without the connections to prove their worth.

Sparky dropped a little cum on their birdbath. He didn't want to lose too much. It was enough to remind him of a dog marking its territory with a little bit of piss. No one would see him unless Sandy found some sort of switch for silence inside himself and sank over the garden walls without destroying anything.

Sparky limped to the shed. The lock and hinges crumbled apart with rust when he looked at them. Anything in the shed wouldn't be useable. The people sleeping away the stresses and worries of the day didn't think much of their past aspirations. More the reason to display it in the garden.

Sparky grabbed a plant. He came prepared for the dust. He

didn't come prepared for the mould. Environmental health needed to see that. It offered a risk to the surrounding houses and alley rats.

Sparky didn't reach in. The mould looked like it was about to grow legs and start walking. It already had teeth.

Sparky moved onto the next garden, hoping Sandy wouldn't spread the mould around. Environmental health would be forced to shut down Suburban Hell until decontamination occurred if Sandy did that. The residents wouldn't be pleased about their special showers.

As much as Sparky would enjoy watching the residents nit-picking each other, he didn't want Papa caught up in it. He didn't want Papa's electronics to be discarded with the hazardous waste. Loss of the keytar would spell his death.

Keytars weren't as cool as guitars, especially because Papa only caught the tail-end of synthpop; he wasn't a pioneer. The other residents would laugh at his tears and eventual suicide. Karen would be pleased with the insurance payout and use it for a prince on the online dating scene.

Karen would have told the unofficial residents' association his dirty little secrets. Men and women sipping tea and hidden bottles of gin in the church hall, sharing shit on each other and complaining. They liked the ammo. It gave them strength and made them feel better about their pathetic little lives.

Sparky would die too, without Papa's cum to fire up his circuits in the night. He didn't want to die. His life was only getting started. He would show Papa how to live again.

The next garden kept the flamingos hidden too, but the garden gnomes were displayed proudly. At least one had been hand-painted by Papa's father.

One lonely lantern lit up the garden. The residents were of similar status to Karen. They must be friends. Papa didn't keep details of Karen's friendships and rivals in his spunk.

Sparky kicked over the lantern and pushed open the door to the shed. The wood cracked with freshness, signifying the owners were rapid climbers. They wouldn't be Karen's friends for much longer.

The contents of the shed didn't have time to collect dust. The varnish smelled new. The stuff held onto the vague hint of loft storage.

Sparky poked a box; out tumbled sewing supplies. It seemed

there was another aspiring fashion designer living on the same street. He or she might have some tape for Sparky's broken foot.

The sewing machine sat on the table, plugged in, cleaned and ready to use. Sparky ran his finger along it. Clean.

Plastic containers of fabric and sewing supplies sat piled from floor to ceiling along the far wall. He moved over to them, losing a piece of plastic from his foot. He bent to pick it up, running his eyes along the containers. In the bottommost centre one, he saw what he was looking for.

Fabric tape wouldn't be as strong as silver tape. It would have to do until he found something stronger. He stacked the boxes on the table, next to the sewing machine. He didn't want to trash a shed when the person it belonged to so obviously didn't want to give up on their dreams.

21

"**What you got** in there?"

Sparky didn't hear Sandy approaching. He nearly dropped the plastic container onto his other foot. He rebalanced and turned around, placed the container on the table, and pointed at the sewing machine with his extendable vacuum-cleaner arms.

"Ha. Ha."

The sound of mechanical laughter made cum seep out of Sparky's eyes. The same cum would be powering Sandy now. It should be seeping from him, too.

"Why do you need sewing supplies?"

Another piece fell off Sparky's foot. He picked it up and reached into the last box for the tape. He rummaged around, finding a few different rolls of various types of craft tape. The owner of the shed was into more than sewing, but sewing seemed to be their favourite.

Something shone at him with the Duck Tape brand stamped across it. He would have to tell Papa "Duck Tape" was a brand of duct tape.

It wasn't silver, but glittery. Beneath his Christmas-tree light eyes, he couldn't tell what colour, or if it reflected objects.

There weren't any scissors in the box. He scanned his eyes around the containers. Someone into sewing would have scissors, numerous pairs. Papa didn't know what the difference was between one type of scissors and the next.

Sparky found a box of scissors and grabbed what appeared to be the sharpest. He put the broken pieces of his foot back on like a jigsaw puzzle. The tape was strong and sticky and difficult to cut.

Sandy's robotic laughter echoed around the shed until the fabric absorbed it. Sparky glared at him, keeping his fairy lights from twinkling. He wanted, more than anything, to tell Sandy to shut the fuck up.

He did it with his eyes, but those were easy to ignore. The way Sparky looked at him must have caused some sort of reaction.

"Chill."

Sandy took a step back with his hands up. They shared Papa's cum. It could have made it easier to communicate. Sparky was having too many difficulties with the roll of tape and scissors, and trying not to let the plastic shards of his broken foot fall off to investigate the matter.

They didn't fit in perfectly. Plastic was easy to break. Parts of the broken pieces fell off, never to be seen again.

Sparky went back to the tape. He managed to cut off a piece, but it stuck to the end. He tried to throw it at the wall. It wouldn't leave his fingers.

The spunk powering him felt Sandy wanting to laugh.

22

"**What seems to** be the problem in here?"

Papa came to save the day (or night). Sparky turned around, pleading flashing in his eyes. He held out his finger with the tape stuck to it.

Papa stepped into the shed. He had a quick look around and took in a deep breath. "Damn."

He turned to Sparky.

"Let's get you fixed up. Then we'll go back to our shed and get you a voice."

Papa took the tape and scissors from Sparky. It took less than five minutes for Sparky's foot to be fixed.

"They're going to know it was me now. You two left semen samples all over the neighbourhood. And now, I've stolen something."

Papa waved at Sparky's foot. He scooped up both robots and left the shed.

"You two caused a stir in the neighbourhood."

Papa took them out of the back gate.

"Everyone is upset. All their hidden dreams they worked so hard to bury are on display for the neighbours to see."

Papa shook his head. "I wish I could see it as a blessing, but people will be out with their pitchforks before long."

"There aren't any pitchforks."

"Vocal pitchforks. Mrs James had a stroke when she woke up to find her ghost hunting equipment on the lawn."

"That's an embarrassing hobby. How did she expect to make a living from it?"

"People do, Sandy."

The Moon poked out from the clouds and shone on Papa's hair.

"Why, Matthew, are you wearing a wig?"

"Hair extensions, glued in with my own cum. Got out my trusty keytar, too. If everyone in Suburban Hell had aspirations, I no longer want to keep mine hidden. Karen can take her garden gnomes and shove them where the sun doesn't shine."

They walked the rest of the way in silence, rats staring up at them. Papa entered their garden.

"It doesn't look like I'll be getting any sleep tonight."

He unlocked the shed and carried both robots inside.

"You behave yourself now."

He put Sandy down on the floor.

He placed Sparky on the table, next to some wires and speakers.

"I can't even wrap my head around you being alive, let alone all the destruction you caused, but look what I found while you were busy breaking and entering."

23

Papa took off Sparky's head and turned it upside down. Sparky felt a sudden rush of light-headedness.

"Just need a moment for the cum to settle."

Papa hummed to himself. Sparky felt exposed as Papa stared into his head. Sandy climbed onto the table and peered inside.

Plastic couldn't go red, but cum could boil. Sparky tried to stop it. He didn't want Sandy to know his humiliation. The spunk bubbled and popped in Papa's face.

Papa let out a good-natured laugh. Sandy's robotic one ruined it. The next cum bubble was one of anger.

"Calm down, now, little guy. I can't operate until the jizz stops boiling."

Sparky watched the world from upside down. Another spunk bubble burst in Papa's face, right on the tip of his nose, spattering him with his own goo. He had to wipe it away and flick it at the wall.

"Calm down, little guy. I need to operate."

Sparky's eyes went dull. He dreamt he was up on stage with his keytar strapped around him. The crowd pushed against the barrier. He looked at the makeup streaming down the faces of the front row. Their hands waved in the air.

The venue filled. He thought people were turned away at the door because capacity had been reached. No one considered people tended to fill out as they aged. The front row was pushed right down to their ribs between their layers of skin and blubber. They waved their arms anyway, happy to be there.

One brave soul took off her bra and threw it at the stage. Security was tight with quick reflexes and pulled it off again. Matthew would have liked to take it home and sew it into a blanket to snuggle at night.

Sweat dripped between the cellulite and bat wings, dragging glitter with it into every skin crater. Matthew's special hairspray would be able to withstand the heat in the room. He styled his hair himself with his own spunk, a precursor of things yet to come. No one else was allowed near it.

The first drop of sweat dripped down Matthew's forehead as he began to play. This was a false memory implanted in Papa's cum, to keep him sane and alive. Papa was never that big.

Sparky felt him tinkering around in his head.

The cum swirled around. Sparky grabbed at it, a combination of broken memories and fantasies. He wanted another trail he could follow before Sandy's eyes brought him to boiling again.

Karen sat on the toilet. A younger Karen, but he could still tell it was her. Matthew went to leave.

"No, you stay. This is your doing."

The sound of urine hitting a clean cup sounded in the room. Sparky felt Matthew's discomfort and sent up a bubble of cum. He needed a different memory to travel. The jizz popped above him and rained back into his head.

"Not long now, little guy, then you'll be able to tell me everything you saw last night."

Sparky wondered why Matthew wasn't shocked that he was alive. Every night, he would spunk into Sparky's backside and wonder why more cum didn't leak out. He didn't realise it powered Sparky through the long and lonely nights.

Sparky's head lifted into the air.

"Hold him there, Sandy, I might need to make a few minor adjustments."

Sparky didn't like the thought of Sandy's hands on him. Despite running on Papa's spunk, Sandy was still destructive. It wouldn't take much for him to drop Sparky's head and spill his spunk, claiming his hand slipped. Residue of his own Papi's spunk would be dusted to his inside and lurking in every crack in his metal and plastic. It would be difficult to undo all that programming.

Sparky chased Papa's semen thoughts. It was better than thinking of what Sandy might do to him. Sparky stopped his lights from flashing. He couldn't close them against the upside-down world. Switching them off, he only saw shadows until he clung onto one of Papa's thoughts deposited in the spunk an hour ago.

Sparky climbed into a picture of a music shop. The keyboards were too heavy to lug around and pretend to be Depeche Mode. Papa's frame was much smaller, until Karen started popping them out.

He didn't eat much, and what he did consume was low in fat. He tried every diet imaginable to stop the oozing, pus-filled boils from taking over his face. No tasty memories lurked in his spunk.

Karen's juices were the most unpleasant of all. She still demanded it every now and again when the batteries in her vibrator died, or whoever she was having an affair with called it off. She always tasted unpleasant. Like something crawled inside her and died, with a faint hint of mould.

Matthew tried to avoid oral, but there were times she demanded it. Memories of a chunk of toilet roll in her pubes caught on Sparky's circuits. The toilet roll was hard. It came off in Matthew's mouth and chipped a tooth. She kicked him in the shins for crying and demanding she wash herself in future. Cum leaked from Sparky's eyes with the memory, dripping onto his upside-down forehead.

Sandy's mechanical laughter echoed around the shed.

"Quiet now, Sandy. I need to concentrate."

"Sorry, Matthew."

Sparky felt Sandy's eyes burrowing into his cum. The thoughts belonged to Papa, not Sparky, but still, Sparky couldn't help but feel violated. He chased Papa's memories, looking for a fantasy.

Papa sat backstage, moaning. Someone with a press pass milked him for the special ingredients for his hair. She'd give him a favourable review if he let her stick her fingers up his arse. There weren't any objections on his part.

He wouldn't let her touch his keytar. The fact she asked meant he couldn't produce the best goo. She had to siphon it out with her mouth and spit it into his palm. He rolled it between his fingers before running it through his hair. It was the most help Matthew would allow. He liked to do everything for himself.

He held the woman's head down with his other hand, only letting her up to spit. Even back then, he had balls that needed a lot of relief.

"That should do it."

Papa took Sparky's head back and flipped it over onto his body. He trailed wires from Sparky's head into his torso.

"Hold still now, Sparky. I need to open your tummy for the speakers."

Sparky sat perfectly still with Sandy's angry eyes watching him. They made him nervous. He reached for his otter and stroked it, feeling each place the moths chewed through its fur and let out a little bit of straw.

He watched Papa using a tiny screwdriver. He used tweezers to thread the wires from his head down to his tummy. The speakers Sparky found in a shed fell out, covered in gooey cum.

Papa laughed. He pulled on the speakers he'd found instead.

"Try to speak before I glue you back together."

"Hello."

Sparky's voice sounded just as robotic as Sandy's. He didn't mind. He was happy to talk. Trouble was, he'd been kept quiet for so long, he didn't know what to say or where to start.

Papa glued him back together in silence.

"Now you have a voice, you don't know how to use it."

Papa threw his head back and laughed.

"It's getting late, I better get back into the house."

Papa handed Sparky his stuffed otter.

"I don't want to know why you took this awful thing, but you obviously like it. Tomorrow, we'll get those new lights wired up on you."

Papa left the two robots in the shed with the door unlocked.

24

"**I** better power down for the day."

Sparky stretched his arms.

"There's still darkness left. Come on, Sparky, don't be a party pooper."

"Nope, I'm staying here. I have what I wanted."

Sandy grabbed at his arms.

"Come on, we both need cocks so no one mistakes us for girls. What did you do with mine?"

"Threw it out. The light didn't work."

"Of course it didn't work. It needs to be attached to me."

Sandy slapped his shoulder.

"You really are a bit slow, aren't you? Matthew not blow his load enough in you? Maybe he's got a bit of a prostate problem?"

Sparky walked away, spunk boiling inside. There wasn't much space. He ended up in a dusty corner with the spiders, fat on Papa's cum.

Sandy pressed the keys on the keytar. It wasn't plugged in, but Sparky didn't like it.

"Stop that. Papa loves that instrument more than anything else in the entire world. Go kick over gnomes or something. I'm going to power down."

Sparky turned to face the corner. He didn't care if cum flakes snowed on him. He didn't want to get Papa into any trouble once Suburban Hell woke up.

Sandy grabbed his arm.

"We're going out. There's enough cum in you to hit another few sheds."

Sparky grabbed the side of the shed. Sandy pulled his legs.

"Come on."

"No. We'll run out of juice."

"I don't care."

"If power fails in someone else's shed, we'll die."

Sandy pulled. Sparky planted his fingers underneath a wooden board. The wood cracked.

"Stop!"

Sparky put as much of Papa's emotion into the scream as he could. He still sounded mechanical. The wood cracked more with each pull.

"The shed is going to collapse."

"No it won't, not if you come with me now."

"No, Sandy. We need to power down. Our circuits need to charge."

"I'm as filled up as a cheap escort."

Sandy pulled. Sparky's Christmas tree lights for eyes lit up. He watched a nail come loose.

"Sandy, I'm serious, the shed is coming apart."

The wood creaked in agreement.

"You're breaking it."

"That makes no sense."

Sparky grabbed another board. The one above had finger slots from the board below being pulled out of place.

"Papa's keytar is in here. He'll be devastated if it breaks."

"He shouldn't leave it alone in the shed."

"But Karen won't let him have it in the house."

"He shouldn't listen to her."

"I'm not listening to you and still, you're making me do something I don't want."

The board ripped from the side of the shed. Sparky landed face-first on the wooden floor. Sandy dragged him by the feet. Sparky dug his hands in, looking for anything to grab onto. Another board, warped by cum, stuck up. Sparky grabbed that.

The table would have made more sense, but it wasn't within reach, despite the extendable arms. Sandy would have ended up dragging both Sparky and the table.

Sparky's legs were secure enough not to rip out. The floorboard, less so.

"Sandy, don't do this. Go away."

Sandy wasn't listening. All that hassle to get a voice and Sandy refused to hear Sparky.

"You don't want to be mistaken for a girl-bot again, do you?"

"It isn't what's on the outside. How I feel on the inside is what counts."

Sparky sweated out cum. Either the shed would collapse, or he would. The board came up in his hands as Sandy pulled on his legs. They should be extendable, like his arms, but Sandy found the spot they stopped at and pulled on that.

The shed moved. Sparky refused to let go.

"Stop it! Papa's keytar will be hurt."

"Papa's keytar will be hurt?"

Sandy laughed his mechanical mocking sound.

"What was the point in getting a fucking voice if you won't listen to me? I don't want to go. I want to stay right here."

"Too bad."

Dried cum snowed onto Sparky and became stuck in the wet man-juice leaking out of him.

The floorboard came away with a final yank from Sandy. It sent a crack running to the wall. It went right up. It was a load-bearing floorboard.

Sparky looked up, the fall of cum-dust blurred his vision, but he could see what he assumed were chunks of wood falling on top of Papa's keytar. He tried to get to his feet, but Sandy pulled him out of the shed.

"We have to save Papa's keytar."

"No, we have to destroy suburbia's secret hopes and dreams."

"Why? What's the point?"

"With everyone miserable and conked out on prescription drugs, we'll be free to raise an army of garden gnomes."

"And the point in that?"

"I haven't thought that far ahead."

Sparky rolled over, extended his arm, and took a swipe at Sandy's legs. Whoever's cum residue resided in Sandy was a purely evil, spiteful person. But even that person knew enough to keep Sandy immobilised.

Wood fell on Sparky. Sandy was clear of the shed. Sparky took another swipe at Sandy, this time at his arms. Sparky had to get up to rescue Papa's keytar. It was the only thing keeping Papa going. Sparky knocked Sandy's arm off. He took a swing at the other one. Sandy let go before Sparky could knock that one off too.

He backed out of the shed. Sparky stood up as the ceiling fell down in a blizzard of cum flakes. He reached Papa's keytar and grabbed it. The thing was bigger than him. He knocked it on the floor dragging it out of there. Papa would need to fix it, but at least the keytar was safe from falling debris.

Sandy reattached his arm while Sparky was distracted.

"You rescued the fucking keytar. Come on, let's get out of here."

"I'm not going anywhere."

"What are the neighbours going to say when they wake up and find a destructive robot in front of Papa's shed clutching a keytar? Frankly, if I were Matthew, I'd be embarrassed about my choice of instrument, but that'll be the least of his worries."

"Everyone has secrets locked away in their sheds, unless their gardens are filled with plastic flamingos and plaster bird baths."

Sandy laughed.

"Dude, it's a fucking keytar!"

"Papa loves his keytar."

"Don't I know it. I'm filled with spunk too."

Sparky turned away. Sandy grabbed him.

"If you don't come with me, I'm breaking into the house to steal Karen's vibrators. We can both have one."

If they did that, the neighbours would know Papa didn't have sex with his wife anymore. Sparky couldn't allow that.

He placed the keytar on the grass. There wasn't a tarp or anything to pull over it and protect it in case it rained. Papa didn't have enough status amongst the neighbours for a garden umbrella. Karen reminded him of that every time it rained on the three barbeques they were allowed to host each summer.

25

By the time Sparky felt satisfied the keytar would be safe, Sandy had already broken into the house. Sparky had never been inside. He was a shed robot.

He knew the layout because it was written in Papa's spunk. In theory, Sandy should be at least vaguely familiar with it. The anger of his previous sperm donor circulated in him, mixing with Papa's cum.

The kitchen tiles gleamed. Karen didn't want to impress the neighbours, she wanted to blind them so they couldn't see she only had one lantern. The scent of floral disinfectant couldn't cover up the smell of spent sperm and Karen's vibrators.

Sparky suspected they were kept in the master bedroom upstairs, but Papa had never seen her use them or put them away.

Sandy ran into the next room. He didn't bother to admire Karen's eye for interior design down a narrow corridor. The mirrors lent the area a sense of light and space against the magnolia walls.

Sandy knocked a vase of plastic flowers. Sparky ran to stop it from shattering. He didn't want Papa and his wife to wake and find the robots routing through their things. It wouldn't be surprising if the shed collapsing had brought them up from dreamland by a few levels. It wasn't a good place for a vase. Memories of Papa knocking it came flushing into Sparky's circuits.

"Be careful."

"Where are the vibrators kept?"

"Turn your volume down. We need to go back outside and wait for Papa to wake up."

"I'm not going anywhere without a new cock."

"We can't get to them."

"I'm going to look down here first. Karen might keep one tucked between the sofa cushions."

"The neighbours would sit on it when she invites them over for tea and gossip."

"I'm going to look anyways."

"No!"

Sparky grabbed Sandy's arms.

"I'm not going to let you."

His mechanical voice cracked with emotion, Papa's emotion, but at least his voice expressed it. Anxiety and anger fought for dominance in the cum running his circuits.

Sparky pulled Sandy back. Sandy turned around and pushed him to the floor. The noise bounced off the walls and up the stairs.

"You'll wake up Karen. The bitch'll come at us with a rolling pin and smash our bodies apart to break the circuits."

"I'll shoot her with my lasers."

"That didn't work this morning, it won't work now."

Sandy pressed the button to fire his laser. The red dot shone on the floor. Nothing else happened.

"See?"

Sparky waved his arm beneath the laser.

"They can't do anything, except perhaps blind someone if you pointed directly at their eye and held it there."

"They can too."

"No, Sandy."

Sparky shook his head. Cum leaked from Sandy's eyes.

"You're just a toy. Nothing more than that."

"But we destroyed people's ambitions together."

"We exposed Suburban Hell's ambitions. We didn't destroy. We brought them out of the sheds and onto the lawns. Really, we're doing a service for people like Papa. But we have to be careful."

"I don't need your lecture."

Sandy pulled away, cum streaming down his face and dripping onto Karen's clean floor. Sparky went into the kitchen. They weren't allowed to move into a house with a utility room, even if they could afford it, but they had a cupboard with a mop and bucket. The floor steamer would make too much noise and wake the post-graduate children sleeping away the day, ready for another day of depressing underemployment in the morning.

Sandy sat on the stairs, trying to slow the tide of cum leaking from his eyes. He made no offer of help. Sparky mopped up the spunk. He couldn't do anything about the stairs, they were carpeted.

"There isn't any point. They'll know we were in here. That Karen knows everything."

"Come on, time to go."

"Not without a cock."

Sparky's eyes flashed. Sandy stood up and ran up the stairs. The carpet muffled his footsteps. It didn't stop Sparky's cum from simmering. They reached the landing.

26

Sandy looked confused. Sparky knew where to go. He didn't believe he'd be able to get Sandy back down the stairs and outside, where they belonged.

"I'll get them."

His volume was down to one on the knob. Sandy let him past.

Sparky cracked open the door of the master bedroom. Karen and Papa snored. They slept, each facing an opposite side of the room.

The vibrators would be in Karen's nightstand. The carpet in the room was thick, to trip up any unsuspecting robots. He wasn't sure Sandy's wheels would be able to withstand the thick shag. That would be a blessing.

Karen didn't allow visitors to view the master bedroom. The high-quality carpet was worth daily doses of sushi through the letter box while she badgered Papa in Majorca for two weeks.

Sparky listened to his cum simmer inside and slight feedback from his speakers. It sounded much louder than it was and he knew that, but his circuits sparked with electricity to make his spunk bubble.

Papa let out a loud snore.

Sparky didn't want to be caught in the house, even though it would be obvious the two robots had been inside once Karen discovered her vibrators missing. Papa might have to serve her pleasure needs until he got her new ones. There was plenty of ball-juice to go around, but Sparky didn't want Papa to put his dick up her. Residue of her juices would get inside and fuck with his circuits.

Sparky stood still and signalled with his hand for Sandy to be slow and quiet. The sound of the carpet would muffle a fall if his wheels couldn't handle it, but Sandy was the sort to cry out in exaggerated pain, which he couldn't feel because he was a robot.

Sandy didn't obey. Sandy pushed past him while Sparky watched the two breathing forms on the bed.

The duvet moved up and down. Someone moved an arm. They weren't in deep sleep. Too much commotion in Suburban Hell for deep rest.

Sandy moved to the wardrobe and swung open the doors. He started to pull out clothes. Sparky knew it would be no use trying to speak to him. It would only lead to an argument to wake up Papa and Karen.

27

Sparky went for Karen's nightside table. Hidden in the bottom drawer, beneath an old real-life woman's magazine, he found baby wipes. The vibrators should be with them.

Sparky looked over at Sandy, pulling clothes off the hangers and throwing them on the floor. It made some interesting confetti when he found Papa's old stage outfits. It could have been worse. It could have been butt rock Papa played.

Sparky shut the drawer and opened the one above it to vibrators. He didn't think the chunks on the used tissues were snot. Karen could have a little robot of her own with that much lady juice, but obviously, she wanted to build a man out of Kleenex and baby wipes.

Sparky grabbed the vibrators and shut the drawer. Temptation called him to run. He ignored it and backed away slowly, tripping over one of Papa's many black scarves. This one had glitter moons and stars. He regained his balance without dropping the vibrators, or creating very much noise.

A few tense seconds passed with his cum simmering away inside him. Everything sounded louder in the dark. Karen and Papa continued snoring, unaware of what transpired in their bedroom.

Sandy pulled more of Papa's clothes out of the wardrobe. The stonewash jeans came next. It looked like he wanted to try to crossover into butt rock territory. Sparky didn't know how much use butt rockers could get out of a keytar player wearing less makeup than them.

"Hey, Sandy, I found the dildos. Put that stuff back."

Sandy either didn't hear him or chose not to. He carried on rummaging and making it rain stage clothes.

"Some of this stuff is ridiculous. How could anyone ever think it was cool?"

"Turn down your volume."

"No."

"For a robot that cared so much about his lack of a cock half an hour ago, you don't seem to care anymore."

Sandy responded by throwing Karen's sequined dress at him. It landed on Sparky's head and became caught in the bucket handle as he tried to remove it. Sparky felt hope drain from his circuits.

He tried to leave the room. Karen would smash them to pieces if she woke up. Let Sandy be smashed alone.

Sandy kept pulling clothes from the wardrobe. Decades' worth of stuff. Karen refused to throw any of her old stuff away "in case it came back into fashion". She never considered that as she aged and popped out children, her hips became bigger.

Papa refused to give up on his dreams, even if those ambitions resided in the shed. He was surprised his wife hadn't sent his stage clothes to live outside with the keytar, too.

Sparky heard the slicing of plastic. Each tear seemed to happen at a time when neither Karen nor Papa was snoring. Cum bubbled upwards inside him. If he were a person, he might vomit.

"What are you doing?"

"I found one of the vacuum seal bags that Matthew's memories only vaguely hint at."

Curiosity peeped up. Papa knew the bags were there, but he didn't know what of his Karen had locked inside them. Sparky put his hands to his ears, still clutching the vibrators, and shook his head. The movement turned them on.

He jumped, forgot about his voice and screamed, and dropped them to the floor. The thick bedroom carpet did nothing to stop the echo. Sparky dove for them. He couldn't find the off button.

The sound of tearing plastic rang on the early morning air. The symphony of sounds could be replicated on a synthesiser much to Karen's nightmares, remixed and make the charts.

Papa rolled over on the bed. A bubble escaped Sparky's mouth.

"Sandy, stop it. Help me."

"I don't care if they wake up."

"Karen'll smash us beyond repair."

"Not now that I have this."

Sandy pulled out a bit of plastic from behind his back.

"What is it?"

"A decent laser. Watch."

Sandy pointed it at the bed. It made a strange noise, but nothing else happened. There wasn't even a red dot.

"I need a moment to get it working. With it, we can take over Suburban Hell."

Distracted, Sparky found himself capable of turning off the vibrators without thinking. Papa's snores evened out while he watched Sandy fiddle with the piece of plastic. Sparky forgot he was standing in Papa's bedroom with a robot still experiencing his previous owner's hateful personality flaws.

"It needs some juice to get it going."

"I don't have any to spare."

"Not that type of juice. Geez, what is it with you? First the dildos and now your mind is fixated on semen."

Sparky thought Sandy would have rolled his eyes if he had the sort that could be rolled.

"I'm not the one obsessed with having a cock."

"Then why are you holding them?"

"I thought that was the point of breaking in."

Karen farted in her sleep. The smell made Sparky's cum boil and forced him to pause. There wasn't any point in arguing with Sandy. The best bet was to resign himself to agreeing and moving on.

He knew better than to let the vibrators fall to the floor. Sandy would want one before long. Sparky swallowed them down for safe keeping.

He stood back to watch Sandy rummage for the juice. Sparky didn't know exactly what it was he was looking for. He thought it best not to offer any assistance.

"Just stand there, why don't you?"

Sandy didn't have a sarcasm knob to turn, but Sparky thought he'd blow a circuit if he tried any harder.

"I don't know what you're looking for."

"We have the same insides. Search inside yourself for the answer."

Sparky didn't think Sandy knew exactly, either. Vague shapes teased him in the white spunk. Something in a bottle, but Sparky didn't think it would be found in the wardrobe.

"Come on, Sandy, it isn't in there."

"You've been against this idea, against me, since the beginning."

"Breaking into the house was stupid. We have what we came for. Come on, before we wake them up."

"Stop being so negative."

Sandy flashed his eyes at Sparky with enough power to chill his cum. They were lasers, but they didn't burn anything. The red light instead lit up the room.

Karen rolled over, releasing more gas. The smell would either wake up Papa or kill him in his sleep.

Sandy grabbed Sparky's wrist. The vibrators rattled inside him as he tried to pull himself away. Sparky was only cheap plastic and some wires and cum. Sandy had metal parts. If Sparky pulled too hard, he'd fall apart. It wasn't so long ago that Sandy put too much pressure on him, dragging him out of the shed.

"We're staying right here. Help me find the juice."

Sparky knew it wasn't to be found in the wardrobe. He knew what juice they were looking for. It wasn't a weapon, but another toy.

"Come on, Sandy, that juice won't do anything except make laminate slippery."

"Yes it will. We can expose everyone. Then Papa will be happy. You want Papa to be happy, don't you? He can fall in love with that film maker on the other side of the alley and have another chance at life."

"It's a bubble gun, Sandy. Papa used it as a prop in a promotional video long ago, before Karen had morning sickness."

"No, we can use it. We can take out the gnomes."

"We'll have more luck kicking them over."

"I don't want to fight."

"Then put down the bubble gun and get out of here. We shouldn't be in the house."

"Matthew, get rid of that thing."

Sparky looked at Karen. It seemed she was talking in her sleep.

"Come on, before she wakes up."

Sparky grabbed Sandy's shoulders.

"Buy that for me," Karen muttered.

Sparky didn't know what item she was talking about.

"She isn't going to wake up."

"She will if you make much more noise."

Sandy dove into the wardrobe. Boxes and hangers crashed. Karen screamed behind him.

"What the fuck? Matthew, wake up."

Sparky ran for the door, tripping over the thick shag carpet. He heard Karen shaking Papa.

"Wake up! There's two of them now! I told you they were out to get me."

"Go back to sleep."

28

Their voices became distant as Sparky made his way down the stairs, dildos bouncing up and down inside him. He was filled with cum. There wasn't any risk of passing out before he arrived outside.

He skidded across the kitchen tiles and out the door. Sandy would be on his own. Sparky had told him to leave. He'd tried pulling him along, but Sandy wouldn't come along.

He kicked over a gnome in frustration. He didn't have a shed to sleep in. That was Sandy's fault too. Life was swell until Sandy came along and ruined everything.

Sparky needed his otter. He stood on top of the rubble, moving things around as quietly as he could. The tail stabbed his fairy-light eye, but didn't ruin the bulb. He grabbed it and jumped off the rubble.

A cum-curdling scream sounded on the air. Sparky stopped in his tracks and stared at the windows, waiting for them to crack. The gnome he was due to kick over next remained intact.

He heard the neighbour's door slam open before it sounded again.

"What's going on over there?"

Another neighbour opened their door.

"You'll be finished in this neighbourhood, Karen. You too, Gary."

The scream sounded again. Karen wouldn't be able to hear the neighbours, unless there were neighbours around the front of the house too. That's where the master bedroom was located.

Sparky stood still. With neighbours lurking about, it was best not to make any sudden movements, least he was discovered. In the shadows, he could blend in with the gnomes. Karen had an excessive amount. It was her father-in-law that supplied most of Suburban Hell with theirs, after all.

Sparky concentrated. He and Sandy were connected by Papa's cum. He might be able to tune into the other robot's thoughts and see what was happening in the bedroom.

More neighbours came outside shouting, each one competing for dominance.

"Why aren't your hobbies on display?"

"You know something about this."

Another scream from the house drowned out all the voices. Sparky didn't want to be wrapped up in this. He only wanted a voice, and for Papa to be happy. But Papa wouldn't be happy unless his keytar was strapped to him.

Next door's motion-sensor lights came on. They were bright enough to light up Papa's garden too. They shone on the keytar.

"Hey, George, come out here. I knew it was him."

A shadow from next door fell over Sparky. The neighbour had pulled up himself to look over the fence.

"There's the keytar."

"What are you talking about?"

"I told you it was the same Matthew."

Another shadow fell over Sparky as the neighbours debated whether it was the same Matthew from that awful band they couldn't remember the name of. Papa's band wasn't awful until he had to leave.

Sparky didn't argue with them or himself. He concentrated on connecting with Sandy, or even Papa's balls. They didn't have eyes, though, and if they did, they'd be staring at Papa's pyjamas. Sparky needed to see as well as hear.

29

The pictures came in hazy waves. Karen's screaming didn't do much to help the connection. Eyes on the back of his body made Sparky's cum boil, which in turn made Sandy boil.

"Get out of my head."

"Matthew, what are they doing?"

Karen was whining now. Somehow, it managed to be worse than her screaming. She clawed at Papa. Sparky would have slapped her if he was physically in the room. He tried to make Sandy move, but all he managed was flipping her off.

"That's vulgar. There's no place in the world for vulgar robots. In fact, there's no place in the world for robots at all."

Papa shook her off and stepped out of the bed before she could cling to him again. He mumbled to himself, but Sandy couldn't make out what he was saying. Sandy still held the toy in his hand. He pointed it at Papa.

"That's a bubble gun. It probably doesn't even work anymore."

"What do you know about this?"

"Goodbye, Karen."

Papa reached into the wardrobe.

"Where's my suitcase?"

Sandy pointed.

"Thank you."

"Where are you going?"

"To speak to a solicitor."

"You can't leave me. I gave you the best years of my life."

"I think you'll find that's the opposite way around."

"I'll be ruined."

"Don't worry. The unofficial residents' association will let you keep your gnomes."

"I'll tell everyone you beat me."

"I don't care."

Papa shoved old stage clothes into his suitcase. He didn't bother with new clothes bought for him over the years as his wife tried to turn him into a respectable person.

Karen screamed again. The noise echoed off the walls and made the bedside lamp shake. Sparky was surprised the adult children hadn't poked their nosey little heads into the room yet.

"My parents warned me about you."

Banging sounded on the front door.

"Hey, are you going to shut up?"

One of the adult children had woken up.

"Your father is leaving us."

"We've seen it coming for years."

Karen's mouth hung open. Sparky wished there was a fly to land in it.

"Everything okay in there?"

"Clearly not," Papa called down the stairs. "I'll be back for the rest of my stuff."

He zipped the suitcase. It only contained stage clothes and a wig. He scooped up Sandy.

"Where's Sparky?"

"I don't know. Outside, I guess."

Papa carried the suitcase and Sandy down the stairs and out the back door. Sparky cut the connection when he saw Papa's face.

"Hey, can I have your autograph?"

"Can you arrange a reunion?"

"Yes to the first, I don't know to the second."

"Matthew, get back in the house. I'm not done with you."

Papa went to the fence.

"Got a pen?"

"Go get one."

"It is him. All this time, there's been a famous person in the neighbourhood."

"Why don't you appear on *I'm a Celebrity, Get Me Out of Here?*"

"Matthew!"

Papa looked at the house.

The neighbour returned with a pen and an old CD. Matthew smiled. The motion-sensor lights shining all over Suburban Hell made it as bright as noon. Papa put Sandy down next to Sparky and his keytar. He went to the fence and signed the CD.

"So, what about a reunion tour? I'd totally be down for that."

"I'll need to speak to the rest of the band."

"Where are you heading?"

"To do something I should have done a long time ago."

"Keep in touch."

"I will."

Karen appeared on the grass. She threw Matthew's CDs at him. He dodged every one of them.

"That's destruction of property."

"You must have known who he was?"

Karen glared at the neighbour. Matthew went into the house. He returned a few seconds later with a carrier bag and started collecting his CDs.

"This is your fault. Fucking little freaks."

Karen kicked Sandy. He flashed his lasers at her. Sparky was next. He grabbed her foot. She fell onto her rear end, much to the amusement of the neighbours.

She made a grab for the keytar. The neighbour jumped over the fence before anyone realised what he was doing.

"Touch that and I'll break your fingers, you nasty, interfering woman!"

Karen started to sob. "If it weren't for him, I'd have the best garden."

"Well, now you have your chance to prove yourself. Goodbye, Karen."

Papa went over to the rubble and grabbed his other keyboard and tucked it under his arm. He shoved synthesiser pieces into his carrier bag. He wouldn't be able to salvage everything.

The neighbour handed him the keytar. He picked up his suitcase. Sandy and Sparky walked behind him.

They had to go through the house again to get to the car in the front. Sandy kicked over the vase of plastic flowers. It shattered on the laminate.

"I never liked her sense of design either."

Papa opened the door and waited for the robots to step out of the house behind him. He shut it. He held his keys in his hand. It looked like he was thinking of taking off the house keys and shoving them through the letter box.

"I'll need to go get more of my stuff. She may not want to see me."

He put them in his pocket as he took out his car keys. He had to put stuff down to open the boot. He didn't put down the keytar. He put in his suitcase first and then the keyboard, with the carrier bag balanced on top.

Papa unlocked the car without closing the boot.

"You two hop in. I've been hiding something."

Sparky and Sandy went into the back seat. They both took a window to watch Suburban Hell come alive as the world turned grey. Sparky stroked dust and shed rubble out of his otter.

Neighbours on the other side of the street hadn't experienced the contents of their sheds being strewn across their gardens. They wiped sleep out of their eyes and marched across the road with tired curiosity.

Karen's screaming didn't seem to bother them, not with all the excited chatter. Papa's exit would give the residents something to talk about for years to come.

Sparky found it strange next door was so praising of Papa. He didn't have the correct number of lanterns for his age. They suspected he was a failed musician. He should have produced scorn. Instead, they wanted his autograph and for him to join a reunion tour.

Papa returned a short time later with a giant amp. He put it in the boot. He still held his keytar. That ended up with a place of honour in the front seat.

His adult children followed him out of the house.

"See you soon, Dad."

"Send me a text to let me know you're safe."

He hugged them.

"We don't get why you didn't leave years ago."

They turned and walked away from the car. They stood on the front step to watch his departure from Suburban Hell.

"Let me just check the airbag."

Karen appeared at the car. Her eyes were puffy with tears.

"I'll never get a new husband now."

"A new husband would stop you from twitching curtains and comparing yourself to the neighbours."

Papa seemed positively jolly as he turned the key in the ignition. He strapped in the keytar and looked over his shoulder.

"You two buckle up back there."

He strapped himself in, waved goodbye to the neighbours that had come out to watch, and drove off into the rising sun. He pulled down his visor.

"I have an old friend who agreed to take us in. Things are different where we're going. No trying to out-do the neighbours. No snobbery. And everything creative."

He switched on the radio to one of his former band's songs.

About the Author

Suitably labelled "The Queen of Filth," extremist author Dani Brown's style of dark and twisted writing and deeply disturbing stories has amassed a worrying sized cult following featuring horrifying tales such as "56 Seconds," "Night of the Penguins," and the hugely popular "Ketamine Addicted Pandas." Merging eroticism with horror, torture and other areas that most authors wouldn't dare, each of Dani's titles will crawl under your skin, burrow inside you, and make you question why you are coming back for more.